Kat's Fall

Shelley Hrdlitschka

D0377274

ORCA BOOK PUBLISHERS

Library and Archives Canada Cataloguing in Publication

Hrdlitschka, Shelley, 1956-
Kat's fall / Shelley Hrdlitschka.

ISBN 1-55143-312-5

I. Title.

PS8565.R44K38 2004   jC813'.54   C2004-901022-0

First published in the United States, 2004
Library of Congress Control Number: 2004101756

Summary: When fifteen-year-old Darcy's mother is released from prison, he finds it is much harder to love than to hate, until he too is accused of a horrific crime.

Orca Book Publishers gratefully acknowledges the support for its publishing programs provided by the following agencies: the Government of Canada through the Book Publishing Industry Development Program and the Canada Council for the Arts, and the Province of British Columbia through the BC Arts Council and the Book Publishing Tax Credit.

Design and typesetting by Lynn O'Rourke
Cover image by Christy Robertson
Printed and bound in Canada.
Printed on recycled paper.

Orca Book Publishers
PO Box 5626, Stn. B
Victoria, BC Canada
V8R 6S4

Orca Book Publishers
PO Box 468
Custer, WA USA
98240-0468

www.orcabook.com

09 08 07 06 • 6 5 4 3

For Danielle (Dani) with love, always.
—S.H.

I would like to thank Beryl Young, Kim Denman, Diane Tullson and Sandra Diersch for their gentle critiquing and encouragement, and Hank Einarson for his continued interest in my work.
—S.H.

MOTHER SENTENCED TO FIFTEEN YEARS FOR DROPPING BABY OFF BALCONY

Plunge Was Not Accidental, Jury Decides

BY SANDY FROST

Sherri Murphy, the 23-year-old Hope Springs woman charged with the attempted murder of her eleven-month-old daughter, appeared indifferent as Judge Forbes sentenced her Thursday to 15 years in prison. Ms. Murphy ignored the jubilant spectators and frenzied media as she was led, handcuffed, from the crowded courtroom.

It was the end of a highly publicized trial in which witnesses testified that Ms. Murphy was an unfit mother, well-known on the streets for her struggles with drug addiction.

During the trial Ms. Murphy admitted that she was ill-prepared to cope with the extra demands of a handicapped baby. However, she denies intentionally dropping her from the balcony, claiming it was accidental, yet refusing to say how the accident occurred. The baby landed in bushes and survived the 20-meter fall with only minor injuries.

The public outcry at the time of Ms. Murphy's arrest was astonishing and unprecedented. The child was born deaf and also suffers acute epileptic seizures, yet the story of her miraculous survival has won the hearts of Hope Springs citizens, stirring up the demand to see justice done.

Ms. Murphy's four-year-old son also lived with her at the time. The two children now reside with their father.

Ms. Murphy will be eligible for parole in ten years.

One

"Wake up, Darcy."

I hear the familiar voice, but I don't respond. Kat stands at the foot of my bed, shaking my leg.

"Darcy!" she says, louder now. "C'mon! Wake up."

She lets go of me and I hear her step around to my side. I sense her leaning over, peering into my face. Her long hair tickles my neck.

"Darcy?" she asks again in that odd, garbled speech of hers. "Are you okay?"

Trying not to breathe, I concentrate on lying as still as I can. Her breath is warm on my cheek.

"I know you can hear me," she says, suddenly grabbing my shoulders and giving me a shake.

I still don't react and go as limp as possible.

She lets go. "Darcy, you're making me scared," she says. The words run together, probably unintelligible to anyone else, but I understand her. I also hear the quiver in her voice. Deciding to make my move, I wait five more seconds and then, wham! I spring up, fling my arm around her shoulders and haul her down onto the bed with me. Screaming, she thrashes about, trying to hit me, but I hold her too tightly. I let her try to battle loose for a minute or two, but when the fight begins to go out of her eleven-year-old body, I relax my hold. She pushes away and we end up lying side by side, facing each other. She's glaring and her chest is heaving from the exertion. She lifts her hands and signs, "That scared me! Don't do it again."

I simply smile my most charming smile.

"Darcy!" she says out loud, but then signs again, "You're mean!"

"Yeah, but you love me anyway," I sign back.

She shakes her head, but the fire leaves her eyes. She sighs deeply, then snuggles closer. I throw my arm around her, enjoying the feel of her silky hair against my cheek.

Kat has been climbing into bed with me since she was just a baby. She thinks I can protect her from all the monsters and bogeymen out there. I wish. She shivers and I realize she's wearing just a skimpy nightie. Our townhouse is freezing this time of year. Dad won't let us turn the heat over sixty degrees. I tug at the tangled heap of blankets, trying to pull some of them over her shoulders. Her warm body wiggles closer and presses up against mine, and for a brief second I allow myself to enjoy the sweet-smelling girl-body beside me...

She leaps out of the bed. "Darcy!"

I feel my face burn. I didn't mean for that to happen. God, she's my sister!

"You're disgusting!" she signs. I swear she's quivering, she's so pissed off.

"Sorry," I sign back. And I am. But how do you explain to a little kid that some things are out of your control?

She stomps out of the room, slamming the door. I pull the blankets over my head.

WE FALL INTO our usual routine, hoping that will make us forget what just happened. It doesn't, of course, but we have to try. I don't know how much Kat knows about guys, but I'm willing to bet she knows more now than she did a few minutes ago.

Kat has some kind of internal clock that wakes her at the same time every day. She gets me up and then usually makes us breakfast. My job is to remind her to take her seizure medication and to get on the special school bus that collects deaf kids and takes them to their school. Dad's been gone for hours already. He's a truck driver and starts work early, but, to be truthful, even if he were here he wouldn't be here, if that makes any sense. He's never learned to sign very well so I have to translate most of the messages between him and Kat. He finds it easier to ignore us. We find that easier too.

I take a quick shower and then find a plate of steaming pancakes on the kitchen table. I look at them closely, wondering if she's planning to poison me after that bedroom incident. "Are those rabbit turds I see squished in there?" I ask, using my hands.

Kat rolls her eyes, but doesn't look at me. I suspect she won't come running to me to protect her from the bogeyman anymore. Huh. Maybe I am the bogeyman.

"Well, are they?" I ask.

"Yeah right, Darcy," she says with her hands, looking at me somewhere down around chin level.

I stab a couple with my fork. With a snap of my wrist they land on my plate. Cutting a minuscule piece from one, I squint suspiciously at Kat, then put it into my mouth. She's still ignoring me. I chew slowly, deliberately, then leap to my feet, letting my chair crash to the floor behind me. I clutch at my neck, eyes bulging. I glance quickly at Kat again, expecting to see some audience appreciation, but it's like I'm not even here. Being my most dramatic self, I die a slow, painful death, slumping to the floor, my eyes staring lifelessly at the ceiling. I jerk once, then shudder for good measure. Eventually I look to Kat again, but she just shakes her head and goes back to eating. I get to my feet, humbled, pick my chair up off the floor and sit down to eat my chocolate chip-studded pancakes.

She really knows how to hold a grudge, that girl. She never used to be like that. I decide to add grudge-holding to my mental list of things about Kat that are changing. Also on it are mood swings, lip-gloss and tiny breasts. I glance at her. She's still ignoring me. I notice once again how pretty she's become. She used to be just plain cute, but that's something else that has changed. Her face has slimmed down, and her light blue eyes are rimmed with thick dark lashes. Her skin is still clear, and her thick, honey-colored hair is brushed smooth. At the rate she's changing she's going to be drop-dead gorgeous in about a week. Maybe it's a good thing that she won't be climbing into bed with me anymore.

I quit my daydreaming when I hear a horn blast outside.

"Quick, the bus is here!" I sign.

Kat jumps up, grabs the lunch bag she's left on the counter and jogs down the stairs to the front door. She slides her feet into unlaced runners, grabs her jacket from the closet and slings her backpack over one shoulder. For one uneasy moment I think she's still too ticked off at me to even say goodbye, but just as she's climbing into the mini-bus she turns and waves. "See you after school, Darcy," she yells.

"Yeah, later," I sign back, trying to disguise my relief.

Scooping up the newspaper that's lying on the top step, I head back to the kitchen. I'm in no rush to get to school. Hope Springs Alternate is relaxed about starting times. There's no point being any other way.

I finish the pancakes and push my plate away. Pulling the elastic off the newspaper, I let it unfold on the table. Instantly those pancakes start backing up my throat.

Staring out from the front page is a picture of Mom, and I swear she's looking me right in the eyes. The caption reads, "Attempted Murderer To Be Given Parole."

Two

*S*lam.

Bowed heads in a nearby classroom snap up as I bang my locker shut, but it can't be helped. If I don't close it quickly, my skateboard will topple back out.

The five students hunkered over notebooks in my room don't look up when I arrive, but Ms. LaRose does. Marie LaRose. How's that for a la-de-da name?

"Good morning, Darcy," she says. "How are you?"

I shrug as I drop into my chair.

She nods and regards me seriously. I ignore her and open my journal to a fresh page. We have to start each morning by writing, a response to some stupid quote that's written on the board. This is Ms. LaRose's idea of creative writing and it's the only subject I do lousy in. It's not because I can't write well—I actually like writing—it's because I won't, and that's because I have to be careful about what I say. My grade seven teacher—who I'm sure hated me—once told us to write a story, and when I did she showed it to the school counselor, suggesting I harbored "pathological leanings". I bet that's the incident which started the ball rolling to get me sent here, the school for social deviants and misfits. She asks me to write a story and when I do, look what happens. Go figure. That's the last time I'll be creative.

The one good thing about Hope Springs Alternate, though, is we can complete the curriculum at our own pace. I could graduate in another eighteen months if I set my mind to it, or I could take my time and attend school for another four years, probably writing stupid responses to famous quotes for that entire time. I've chosen option A and am flying through my courses. I know Ms. LaRose is impressed. What I don't think she gets is that I'm not doing it to impress her.

Feeling her eyes still firmly fixed on me, I finally look up. "What?" I ask.

She gives her head a shake, as if bringing herself back to the present. "Sorry," she says, "I didn't mean to stare. My mind was just wandering, you know how it is."

Yeah, I do, thanks to her. With her skintight jeans, high heels and low-cut, snug sweaters she looks more suitably dressed to work the streets than to teach way-ward teens.

"By the way, Darcy," she says, interrupting my thoughts. "There's been a meeting called today for you, myself, Mr. Bryson and Ms. Wetzell. We're meeting in this room, after school."

Now that gets my attention. "But I haven't done anything wrong."

"Of course you haven't, Darcy," she answers in her sweetest, most rose-like voice. Her demeanor is in complete contrast to her get-ups. "It's just some kind of midterm evaluation." She glances self-consciously at the others, who have suddenly taken notice of our conversation. I hear Troy—class thug—snicker. Everyone knows she's lying. This is not the way midterm evaluations are done around here.

Out of the corner of my eye I can see Gem, the girl who sits at the next desk, staring at me. I turn abruptly and stare back, expecting her to act properly embarrassed and look away. But she doesn't. Instead she winks and smiles. What's with these people?

"I'm busy," I tell The Rose. "I have a job after school."

"Okay, then how about lunchtime? Should I try to have it rescheduled for noon?"

"I guess." What else can I do? These kinds of things don't go away on their own. I can't for the life of me figure out what this meeting could be about. I bust my butt to stay out of trouble, and it isn't easy. But I have to, for Kat. She depends on me to be around for her. Once you get expelled from this school, the next option is to be sent to the quasi-military one about a hundred miles away.

I shake my head and write out today's quote. *Do not go where the path may lead, go instead where there is no path and leave a trail.—Ralph Waldo Emerson*

Now, I know exactly where Ms. LaRose would like us to go with our response. That's the reason

I won't. This is as close as I ever come to making waves around here.

This Ralph guy obviously hasn't heard that other famous quote, the one that goes "tread lightly on the earth" or something like that. If we all went around tromping through the forest, just think of the mess we'd leave!! And by the way, is this guy the same Waldo as in the Where's Waldo books?

JUST BEFORE OUR morning break, Ms. LaRose comes up beside me and rests her hand on my shoulder. She leans over and peers at my work. The smell of her perfume triggers a strange kind of memory, not of an event, but of a sensation. I try to get a handle on what it is, but it's too elusive. It frightens me. I've had it before and it always leaves me with a pitiful ache in my gut. I jerk my shoulder away. She can go be compassionate somewhere else.

"Can I see your journal please, Darcy?" she asks.

I hand it to her. She reads my entry and laughs. "Nice try, buddy. Now try again. And have it done before the break."

I try again. Sometimes this goes on three or four times before she gives up on me.

I disagree with this Ralph guy's suggestion. It makes more sense to stay on a path that is proven to go somewhere. Why break your back making trails that may only lead to dead ends?

I show The Rose my second entry just as the buzzer sounds for the break. She nods thoughtfully. "Kinda like 'better safe than sorry'," she says.

"Kinda like."

"You're entitled to your opinion," she says, handing me back my notebook.

MOST OF THE kids from my class head straight off the school property to smoke. I wander down to the library where we can borrow CDs. Our librarian's pretty cool, for a teacher. He has a sweet collection of CDs to choose from. I make my selection, snap it into my Discman and settle back in a lounge chair.

"Hey, dickhead!" I hear over the music. I turn the volume up and keep my eyes down.

"I'm talkin' to you, Fraser."

I sigh and pull off the headset. Troy and his two Troy-groupies loom ominously over me. "What do you want?" I ask and then notice the newspaper Troy has rolled up under his arm. Shit! That's what the meeting's all about! How could I be so stupid? I'm not the only one who's seen today's lead story.

"We're just wondering what you think about the news," Troy says, holding the newspaper in front of me and tapping my mother's picture with his nicotine-stained finger.

I shrug and slide the headset back on my head.

Troy reaches over and tugs it off. He reeks of tobacco. "I asked you a question, Darcy. Are you excited about seeing your mommy again?"

"I don't plan to see her," I tell him. "Now get lost."

He stares at me for a moment. I stare right back. "Better stay away from balconies," he sneers. He turns and gives one of his buddies a shove. The buddy swings his arms around and around and sways on his tiptoes, as if to keep from falling. Then Troy gives him just a little flick of his finger and the other guy falls with a thud. The whole scene appears rehearsed.

I put the headphones back on, trying to cover up the sound of their laughter. I sense rather than see them move out of the library and back down the hall. My right hand slides up my left sleeve and I softly stroke the web of threadlike scars on my skin.

ONCE THE OTHER kids are shooed out of the classroom and we are assembled around a table, Ms. Wetzell starts our meeting.

"So, Darcy," she says, looking directly at me. "We have received word that your mother will be released from prison soon." For a person trained in counseling, she is amazingly blunt.

"Yeah," I mumble. "I read that in the morning paper too."

"You read it in the paper?" The Rose asks. "That's how you found out?"

"It's as good a way as any," I say.

I see her jaw clench as she folds her arms across her chest. That's the thing about Marie LaRose. No matter how many times I brush her off, she never quits on me. It's eerie.

"Have you considered how the community is going to react to that news?" Ms. Wetzell asks. Her starched white blouse and pleated navy skirt reflect the no-nonsense approach she brings to her work.

"No," I answer honestly. "It never crossed my mind."

"Well the thing is this," she says, leaning forward and placing both hands on the table. "There's bound to be an uproar. People are going to think she should serve the entire sentence for her crime. As you know, even in prison she's been kept away from the general population, for her own safety."

I hate it when people start sentences with "as you know." If that's so, why say it? "No, I didn't know," I say.

"Oh," she says, looking surprised. But it doesn't take her long to compose herself. It never does. She's the queen of composure. "Well, she has. But once she's released she's going to have to face the music."

"The music?" I ask. A drumroll plays in my head.

"You know what I mean," she answers. "The community is going to let her know how it feels about what she did."

I nod.

"Our concern today," Mr. Bryson, principal of Hope Springs Alternate, says, "is for your well-being." He's been uncharacteristically quiet, but suddenly he pulls his hands out of the pockets of his faded jeans, places them on the table and leans forward.

I can't help but wonder what the hands-on-the-table thing is all about.

"Things could get…difficult," he continues, "and we want you to know that we're here to support you in any way we can."

"Thanks," I say. Like I'd ask *them* for help.

"We don't want the inevitable uproar to be detrimental to the progress you've been making."

Detrimental to the progress? What's that got to do with my well-being? If he could see my arm he might not think my *being* was so *well*. Mr. Bryson, with his laid-back, relaxed attitude, usually scores pretty high on the coolness scale around here, but he's not scoring any points with me today.

"I don't see why it should," I answer, hoping to bring this useless meeting to a quick end.

"Maybe because you're her son?" suggests Ms. Wetzel. I'm surprised by the hint of sarcasm in her voice.

"That may be so," I say. "But I have no plans to associate with her. And my sister won't either, for obvious reasons. So I appreciate you organizing this little get-together, but I really don't think you need to worry."

The three of them stare at me and then glance at one another.

"You don't seem too concerned," Ms. Wetzell says, flipping through the pages in my file. I wonder if she's looking for the document that explains why I was sent to this school in the first place. It's not the cutting, because no one, except Kat, knows about that. My antisocial behavior all through elementary school always concerned my teachers, but I still think it was that paranoid grade seven teacher who clinched my deportation from the regular system.

"I guess I just don't believe in putting out fires where there are none," I tell Ms. Wetzell.

"Oh, I expect we'll see some fireworks where this case is involved," Ms. Wetzell says, slapping my file closed. "And I expect it will be quite a show."

Jumping my skateboard over the curb, I wheel into the Kippensteins' driveway. I didn't mention to The Rose that my job is baby-sitting. That would have seemed way too wussy by the standards of most of the Alternate kids, but it works for me. The thing is, the Kippensteins have a little deaf kid, Samantha, and they need a hearing sitter who can sign. I'm perfect for the job. Not only that, but Kat is welcome to join me. The Kippensteins don't seem to mind that our mom's in jail. I guess they figure being murderous is not a trait you inherit.

Mrs. K leaves for work at four o'clock in the afternoon Tuesday through Friday, and Mr. K doesn't get home until seven o'clock, so that leaves a few hours that Sammy needs to be taken care of. They both work all day Saturday, and I wish they'd hired me for that day too, but Sam has an aunt and uncle who are willing to take her then. The best part of this whole deal is that Kat and I have somewhere to hang out four afternoons a week—keeping us out of Dad's way. Mrs. K leaves dinner ready, and there is always enough for us. I get paid for this. What could be a better arrangement, aside from doing the Saturdays as well?

The deaf kids' mini-bus has dropped Kat off and I find the two girls squatting on the driveway, sharing a big bucket of sidewalk chalk. Their backs are turned to me so I step off my board and watch them for a moment. Kat's long hair sparkles in the winter sunlight, and she's engrossed in the picture she is drawing. Four-year-old Sammy is imitating Kat's every move. I feel a stab of worry for Kat. How are these fireworks that Miss Manners was talking about going to affect her? Knowing the mentality of some of the people in this town, I expect Kat will get drawn in somehow.

Sammy spots me first, drops her chalk and scrambles over to greet me. I grab her under the arms and twirl her around. When I put her back down she squeezes my legs in a tight hug. She reminds me of Kat at that age, but unlike my sister, who was born deaf, Sammy lost her hearing about a year ago during a life-threatening battle with meningitis.

Sammy grabs my hand and tugs me over to see her artwork. "Wow!" I sign and say simultaneously. Her responding grin is the best thing that has happened to me all day.

"Hi, Kat," I sign to my sister.

"Hi," Kat says, giving me a quick glance before returning to her chalk drawing.

I nudge her with the toe of my shoe. She looks up. "How was your day?" I ask.

She shrugs. "Same as always," she replies. With a sinking heart I realize she's still mad at me. She usually has a million little stories to tell about school. Kat notices Sammy's puzzled expression and repeats herself with her hands. We "talk" slowly in front of Sam, trying to help her learn the language.

Watching the girls draw, I wonder, for about the millionth time, what it must be like to live in a silent world.

After a while, Sammy drops her chalk on the driveway. She climbs to her feet and wraps her arms around herself.

"Are you cold?" I ask her, using my hands.

She nods.

"Then let's go in," I suggest and point at the door.

Kat has already finished collecting the pieces of chalk, and she snaps the lid on the bucket.

Mrs. K meets us in the doorway. She puts her coat on as we take ours off.

"Samantha's had a busy day," she tells me as she gets ready to leave. "Make sure, won't you, Darcy, that she's had her dinner and her bath before her dad gets home. That way he can put her right to bed."

I promise to do that and then ask, using my hands *and* my voice, "What should I give her for dinner?" Samantha's not the only one who needs practice with sign language.

Mrs. K smiles at me, fully aware of what I'm doing. "The lasagna is in the fridge," she signs slowly, spelling out the word lasagna. "I left the directions on the counter."

I agree to follow them and hold the door open for her. She tends to hesitate right before she leaves, as if she thinks she might have forgotten to tell me something. I notice Sammy gets tense at this point too, picking up on her mom's anxiety, and she's getting a little worse each day, so the sooner I can get Mrs. K out the door the better. Today Mrs. K seems more fretful than usual, but as it turns out, it isn't the evening routine she's worried about.

"Darcy," she says, even though she has one foot out the door already. She's making no effort to sign. In fact, she's turned her back to Kat so that there's no risk my sister will read her lips. "I saw the morning newspaper. I read about your mom."

My heart sinks. It starts already.

"Are you ready to deal with it?" she asks.

"I'm not dealing with anything," I answer. "Nothing is going to change."

"Really?" she asks, sounding downright skeptical.

"Really," I answer, trying to sound confident.

"Because, you know, I've got Samantha to consider and all…"

So that was it. She might not think there is a murder gene you can inherit, but she does think the murderous mother might suddenly endanger every small deaf girl in town, especially the one the son is babysitting.

"If you're uncomfortable with me watching Sammy because my mother has been released from prison," I say, looking her directly in the eyes and forcing her to look back, "I'll understand. No, actually, I won't understand," I correct myself. "But I'll quit, if that's what you want me to do."

"I don't want you to do anything like that," she says, unable to meet my gaze any longer. She studies the artwork on the driveway. "I've told you that I think you and Katrina are wonderful with Samantha. I just wanted to know what you thought, that's all."

"I think everyone is making a big deal out of nothing," I say, trying not to sound as angry as I feel. "And I think you should go quick," I say, looking around, "while Samantha's preoccupied."

With one last apologetic glance in my direction, Mrs. Kippenstein hurries to the carport and climbs into her Honda Civic. I watch as she backs it out of the driveway and onto the road. With a beep of her horn, she's gone.

I wish I could make my anger disappear as quickly. With a heavy heart I shut the door and go look for the girls.

EVERYTHING'S SET. Kat and Dad are asleep. My Swiss army knife lies ready on my desk in front of me. The towel, stained a deep burgundy from past sessions, is right beside it. I wait, savoring the moment. Then I slowly pick up the knife, press the tip of it into the soft skin on the underside of my arm and watch for that first bubble of blood. I drag the knife across my skin, watching the red line trail behind it. The knot in my stomach that's been gradually growing tighter all day begins to loosen already. I watch the blood pool up, not wiping it off until it runs together, forming a stream that threatens to drip onto my desk. Once the bleeding begins to subside, I poke the tip of the knife into a fresh patch of skin and begin again.

Three

It's Saturday morning. I find a note from Dad propped up among the dirty dishes on the kitchen counter. *Gone shopping*, it says in his barely legible scrawl. Dad's not a man to waste words, so I'm surprised he's left a note at all. I should feel flattered.

When the fridge and cupboards are practically bare, Dad takes Kat to the grocery store. They don't need to talk much to shop. He doesn't like to take me along because a hungry fifteen-year-old boy tends to fill the cart too full. Kat selects food the two of us like to eat. I don't know what Dad eats because we rarely have meals together, and even on weekends he often goes out with his truck-driver friends. I suspect he lives mainly on fast food, judging by the size he's become.

I quickly see why they decided to go shopping this morning. There's only a couple of crusts left in the bread bag, but I pop them in the toaster anyway. Finding no glasses in the cupboard, I look for an almost-clean one on the counter. I rinse it out, pour in drink crystals from a can and fill it with water. I have to really scrape the sides of the jar to get enough peanut butter to thinly cover my two lousy pieces of toast.

Dad's left today's newspaper on the table. My first impulse is to ignore it, a good strategy for avoiding any more nasty surprises, but curiosity gets the best of me. It's like driving by roadkill and not wanting to see but having to look anyway.

The front page is typical. The lead story covers the latest scam in municipal politics. Big hairy deal.

I slowly flip through the pages and when I see no mention of Mom, a flicker of hope begins to brighten my mood. Maybe the story of her release is old news already. But then I hit the week-in-review section. Hope springs daily? Yeah right. My heart sinks, totally. They've given over the whole section to the community's response to Mom's parole. The number of letters to the editor is staggering, and the sentiment is unanimous: Mom should not be set free. Ever. And especially not in this town.

People have written in to say she does not deserve to be forgiven. Some crimes (this being one of them) should never be given early release, or release period, says one law-abiding Hope Springs citizen. There is even the suggestion that the citizens should unite and drive her out. Where, they don't say. One writer went as far as to suggest that a formal protest be planned for outside the prison, and he invited others to contact him to set it up.

It goes on.

A woman calling herself "A Worried Mother" implies that none of the town's children will ever be safe again. Another suggests that her release might be a good thing. Then the community will be able to see true justice done—through some kind of vigilante retaliation. That sends a shiver down my spine.

I'm still reading when I hear Dad and Kat bang through the door. Dad's puffing. He's got four over-flowing bags hanging from each hand. I guess he doesn't want to make two trips to the car. Kat follows him in with a couple of packages.

His glance takes in what I'm reading and he says, sounding oddly pleased, "It's causing quite a stir, isn't it?" He pushes the bags onto the counter, sending the assortment of dirty dishes crashing. Spilt juice and cold coffee stain the papers lying there. I jump up and snatch Kat's report card out of the pile.

"It'll blow over." I try blotting the paper with a dish towel, but it's pointless. I don't know why I care. No one but me reads it anyway.

"Maybe, maybe not."

Kat comes over, oblivious to who and what we are talking about, and pulls some clothes out of the bags she's carrying. I can see that they are not new, probably bought at the second hand store in the same strip mall as the grocery store, but Kat seems pleased with them. She holds a blue sweater up in front of her. Her eyes ask the question, "Well?"

Tucking the report card under my arm, I nod my approval and tell her, with my hands, that the blue matches her eyes. I can see she is pleased. "What else did you get?" I ask.

She pulls an assortment of jeans and shirts from the bags and I have to agree, she did do well. They must have had a new shipment of donations recently.

Dad goes into the living room, flops down on the couch and flicks on the TV. "Darcy," he calls back to me. "Could you ask your sister to make us some brunch?"

I guess he's not planning to put the food away, but I should be grateful. At least he brought it in from the car.

I'M UNPACKING THE last bag when the phone rings.

"May I speak with Darcy Murphy?" the voice on the other end asks.

Alarm bells go off in my head. I go by Fraser, my dad's surname. Murphy is my middle name, after my mom. Whoever is calling obviously wants to talk to my mom's son. I don't want to talk to anyone who connects me with her. Not knowing what to say, I hang up the phone.

It rings again a moment later. I see Dad glance up from the couch in the living room.

"I'm sorry," the same voice says when I pick it up again, "somehow we got disconnected."

"There's no one here by that name," I answer.

"How about Katrina Murphy?" he asks.

"Nope. She doesn't live here either." I hang the phone up again.

"Who was it?" my dad calls from the living room.

"Wrong number," I call back to him.

When it rings again I stare at it. I can feel Dad staring at me. It keeps ringing, three, four, five times.

"Pick it up!" Dad orders.

I don't do anything.

"What are you, daft?" he hollers while heaving himself off the couch. He storms into the kitchen. Before he reaches the phone I pick it up and just as quickly slam it down. He stares down at me incredulously.

I see Kat watching us from the stove, where she has just cracked eggs into a sizzling frying pan.

"It was someone who wanted to talk to Darcy Murphy," I explain.

"Yeah, so? That's your name. Why didn't you talk to them?"

"You know damn well why I didn't talk to them," I answer.

"No, I don't," he replies. "You have no idea what they wanted."

"I know it has something to do with Mom, and that is reason enough not to talk to them."

It's a standoff. He glares down at me. I stare right back at him. Kat flips the eggs.

The phone rings again. This time my dad snatches it before I even have a chance to move. "Hello?" he says, still staring at me.

I watch his face as he listens. His expression has changed from its bully-the-kid look to an I-like-what-you're-saying-and-tell-me-more one.

"Uh-huh," he says. "Yes, I'm the father." He glances at me and then returns to the living room with the phone at his ear.

I follow him.

"Of course we can talk to you. Yes, it has been hard, but I've done my best. She's fine. No, there was no permanent damage. A photographer, too? Sure, bring one along."

I stand in front of him and wave my arms. "No, Dad," I say. "We're not talking to anyone!"

He turns his back to me. I move around in front of him again.

"This afternoon would be fine," he says.

"No, it isn't," I say as forcibly as I dare.

"Around three o'clock?" he suggests.

"I won't be here," I say to him.

"We'll see you then," he tells the speaker and shuts off the phone.

We're back to our standoff, but this time it's me doing the glaring. He's looking slightly amused. I'm just about to say something I would definitely have regretted later, but there is a crash in the kitchen.

"Kat!"

I wheel about and race across the room. In the kitchen I see her leaning over the sink, shaking violently. The frying pan has been knocked off the stove and the eggs have left greasy snail-trails where they've slid across the floor.

Being careful not to step on any of them, I gently lift her rigid body and carry her back to the living room, where I lay her on the same couch Dad has just vacated. I cover her with the blanket that we keep there for TV watching. Her eyes are rolled back in her head and she is sweating profusely, yet she's shivering at the same time.

"Find me a clean dish towel," I tell my dad. Actually, it's an order.

He does, and I roll it up and manage to jam it between her clenched teeth to keep her from biting her tongue.

I sit with her, wiping the sweat from her forehead. Dad's leaning against the doorjamb that leads to the kitchen.

"A perfectly good breakfast ruined," he says, glancing into the kitchen.

"Why didn't you remind her to take her pill this morning?" I ask him. We've been down this road before.

"How should I know when she takes it?" he answers. "If you'd got your sorry butt out of bed…"

"She's your daughter!"

"Yeah, well, I won't have to deal with this much longer."

I look at him, trying to take his meaning. "You don't mean…"

"Listen, Darcy. You know I'm not cut out for raising kids. I've done the best I can, given the circumstances. You can stay if you want," he says, grudgingly. "You're almost grown anyway. But if your mom wants her back," he gestures at Kat and makes a face, "I'm not going to stand in her way. You know how this kind of stuff grosses me out."

I stare at him, stunned.

"A girl needs a mother," he continues, sounding like he's trying to convince himself as well as me. "She's going to be going through those difficult years soon, and I don't know what to do with a teenaged girl."

"Probably the same as you do with your teenaged boy," I say. Which is nothing, I think, but don't dare say aloud.

"I'm sure your mom will be completely reformed," he says. "Kat will be better off with her."

"Mom dropped Kat off her balcony, Dad! Doesn't that tell you anything?"

"Of course it does. I was as shocked as the next person. I was sure she loved you guys…"

"Yet you still want to send us back to her?"

"It's not like she'd do that again," he says.

"No, I guess not," I say, noticing that Kat's body is relaxing. I pull the towel out of her mouth. "We're a bit too big now."

Dad comes into the room and sits across from us, in the armchair. "I know I haven't been the greatest of parents," he says, actually sounding contrite.

"No? What makes you say that?"

"Don't get sarcastic on me now, Darcy."

"Well we didn't ask to get born, Dad. But we did. And you're the only parents we have. So how am I supposed to act when one parent tries to kill my sister and the other doesn't even want us?"

He takes a deep breath and lets it out slowly, but he doesn't say anything.

"I might be able to understand it if you'd just had me," I say, deciding now is as good as any time to air a few things that have always ticked me off. "Anyone can make a mistake once, but you went on to have a second kid."

"That was your mother's doing. She swore to me she wouldn't get pregnant again." He sits still, lost in thought for a moment. "You know, things weren't too bad after she was born," he continues finally. "We had one of each—a boy and a girl. Life was okay for a while. I even thought we might get married and lead some kind of normal life, whatever that is."

"So what happened?"

He thinks for another minute before answering. "One day she realizes your sister is deaf. Your mom was always borderline crazy anyway, but that seemed to push her over the edge." He lowers his voice. "I won't swear to it, but I think she may have shaken her a little too hard." He is looking at Kat.

The awful truth dawns on me, slowly. "That's what caused the epilepsy?"

He just shrugs. "That's when I got out of there," he says. "There was no living with her anymore."

I feel the anger welling up, and suddenly I hate her even more, if that's possible. Mom was exposed to German measles when she was pregnant. That's what caused Kat to be born deaf. She couldn't help that, but if she's responsible for the epilepsy—maybe she does deserve to be jailed for life. Or longer.

KAT IS ·EXHAUSTED after the seizure, so she goes to bed. I clean the kitchen and put the rest of the food away. Dad's gone out, probably to get some breakfast. It didn't occur to him to make his own.

My plan is to be out of here before the newspaper people show up, but I don't want to wake Kat. Keeping one eye on the clock, I begin to pace the hall outside her room. I'd like to leave while Dad is still out, but I don't want to leave her here for the big interview. Mind you, without me here, no one will be able to talk to Kat. Dad will look like the fool he is, hardly able to communicate with his own daughter...

I grab my skateboard and head for the door.

I DON'T RETURN until I'm sure they'll be gone, which is after five o'clock. There aren't any suspicious-looking cars parked in front of our townhouse so I climb the steps tentatively. Dad's going to be steamed. I remind myself that he's never been physically abusive, but a little voice in my head keeps telling me that there's always a first time. I wonder how Kat has fared. I hope she realizes I did this for her own good.

The door bangs open. He's waiting for me.

"Where the hell have you been?" he demands before I even reach the top step.

"Out."

"You knew the guys from the paper were coming at three o'clock."

"And you knew I wasn't talking to them." His presence is enormous, it fills the whole doorway, but

I slink past him and into the kitchen. I need to find Kat, make sure she's all right.

"You little bastard!" he says, following me. "Do you know how stupid I looked?"

"That's not my fault."

He looks down at me incredulously. "Then whose fault is it?"

"Yours. You invited them here even though I said I wasn't talking to them. I'm not just some little kid you can kick around, you know."

His face is purple and his fists are clenched. He reminds me of a bull who has just entered the ring at a bullfight—he's exhaling in angry little snorts. I expect to see him start pawing the ground any second.

"Where's Kat?" I ask, craning my neck to look into the living room.

It's as if he doesn't hear the question. "They'll be back here a week from next Wednesday, at 6:00," he says. "And you better be here too. Or else."

"Or else what?"

His eyes are narrowed. "Or else I take back that offer to let you stay on. You'll go back to your mother as well."

That's the ultimate punishment and he knows it. I stare back at him, unable to speak. Eventually I remember Sammy. "I can't. I baby-sit Samantha. You know that."

"Tough," he says, some of the anger leaving his face when he realizes he's got me where he wants me. "You can call in sick for once. And you watch what you say to those newspaper guys. You tell them all about how well we've done for the past ten years, but how you're willing to forgive your mom now. She's paid for her crime, you'll say, and just in time too, because Kat needs her mother."

I really do feel sick. "Where is Kat?" I ask again, desperately needing to get away from him.

"In her bedroom. With the newspapers. I figured it's about time she found out what's going on. And, of course, you weren't here to break it to her gently."

For a second I figure it might be preferable to live with a murderous mother than a heartless father. I rush down the narrow hallway to Kat's bedroom and burst in. She's sitting on the floor with the newspapers spread out around her. Her eyes are red and swollen and she's clutching her favorite stuffy, a tan-colored dog that vaguely resembles a golden retriever. I remember buying it for her when I got my first paycheck from the Kippensteins'.

"Oh, Kat," I say, slumping down beside her. I try to put my arm around her shoulder but she shoves me away.

"That's not why you said she was in prison," she signs. "You said it was because of the drugs."

"I know. But the truth is so awful I thought I'd wait till you were older."

She thinks about that and then her face crumples as a fresh onslaught of tears overcomes her. "I am older!"

IT'S BEEN A brutal day. I feel like crying now too, but, of course, I don't. I'd never cry in front of Kat, or anyone else for that matter. But I know I won't be able to resist the Swiss army knife again tonight. "I guess I should have told you."

She doesn't answer, but she must sense her big strong brother is on the verge of losing it, because she places the box of Kleenex between us. I ignore it.

"What's going to happen now?" she asks after a few minutes.

"I don't know for sure." I consider sparing her any more horrible truths, but decide it's time for complete honesty. "When she gets out of prison, Dad thinks you should live with her. He thinks you need a mother."

She looks up at me, alarmed. "Are you serious?"

I nod.

"What about you?"

"He says I can stay because I'm older. And I'm a guy."

I watch her face as she tries to digest this.

"Do you remember her at all?" she asks finally.

I have to really think about that. I don't remember a lot, but I do remember certain little things, like the warm curve of her body as I cuddled up to her on the couch while we watched TV, or while I watched TV. She was usually asleep—a drug-induced sleep I realize now. And I remember being a little ticked when Kat was born. Mom never seemed to have time for me after that. She cried a lot then too. Kat seemed to make her sad. And, of course, I remember the fall…

"Yeah, I remember a bit," I sign. "She seemed to really love you. I don't know why she did it," I add, thinking that if Kat really is going to get returned to her, I'd better not describe her as the total bitch that I've come to imagine her as. "I think it must have been the drugs she was doing. She was out of control."

Kat stares at her picture. "You look like her," she says with her hands.

"So do you."

Kat begins to tidy up the newspaper. She's still sniffing, but I admire the tough façade she's put on.

I stretch out on her bed, arms under my head, and stare at the ceiling. There's a big water stain directly above the bed, and only a plain lightbulb hanging in the center of the room. The light shade got broken years ago and Dad never bothered to replace it.

I can't bear the thought of being separated from Kat. My life has revolved around her for so long. But I feel equally strongly about not living with Mom. I can never forgive her for what she did. And if she goes back to using drugs when Kat is with her, I don't know what I'll do. Possibly kill her.

Maybe there is a murder gene after all.

Kat plunks herself on the bed beside me, and I see her glance at my arm, but before I can pull it out from behind my head, she's reached over and pulled my sleeve back. I yank my arm away, but not before she's seen the fresh cuts.

"You promised me, Darcy," she says, her eyes filling with tears again.

I sit up. "It's no big deal," I tell her, pulling my sleeve back down.

"Yes, it is," she signs. "You scare me when you do that."

Just like I scare myself. I wish I understood why it helps. All I know is that it does. "I'm in control," I tell her. And that, I know, is true. I am in control of the cutting. It's everything else I'm not in control of, and that's what's scary.

Four

I feel disorientated and groggy when I wake up. My room is too bright. I try pulling my blanket back over my head, willing the day to go away. I notice the throbbing in my arm and feel a little queasy at the memory of the fresh cuts I made last night.

An odd noise coming from the bathroom brings me out of my sleepy stupor. I check the clock. It's after nine o'clock! Where the hell is Kat? Her bus will have come and gone an hour ago!

Pulling on sweatpants, I stumble down the hall and realize that the odd noise I hear is actually heart-wrenching sobs. I find Kat curled up in a corner of the bathroom. She's in a housecoat and her knees are drawn up to her chest. Her face is blotchy from crying. My first thought is that the truth about what Mom did to her has finally sunk in. Or maybe it's the realization of what it would mean to go live with her...

I squat in front of her but she turns away. Grabbing her chin, I turn her head so she has to look at me.

"What is it? Are you sick?"

She yanks herself away and continues to sob.

"Kat!" I say, grabbing her chin again. "You have to tell me what's wrong!" She doesn't need to hear to know what I'm saying. She glances at me, and in that moment I see the terror in her eyes.

"What is it, Kat?"

She drops her face onto her knees and her shoulders heave. I'm at a total loss. I grab those skinny shoulders and give her a little shake, but remember, as I'm doing it, what Mom did to her all those years ago. I let go of her and move away.

Finally, she looks up at me, sitting helpless on the edge of the tub. She signs, "I'm bleeding." Then she begins to wail again.

Bleeding. I think of the blood-soaked towel I shoved under my mattress last night. I squat down in front of her again. "Where are you bleeding?" I sign in front of her face.

She shakes her head from side to side. She's not going to tell me.

I persist. "Kat, how can I help you if I don't know where you're hurt?"

She finally gives in and picks up a pair of pajama bottoms from a pile of clothes tossed on the floor beside her. She holds them in front of me, and I can see that the crotch is covered in blood.

Why would she be bleeding there? A horrible thought takes hold of me. "Kat," I say, taking her by the shoulders again and forcing her to look at me. I speak slowly. "Did Dad do something?"

"Nooooooo," she wails. I have no idea if she knows what I'm talking about, but at least I know it has nothing to do with Dad.

"Then…" I stare at her. She's not old enough, is she? She's only eleven. Oh my God!

"I think I'm dying!" she wails.

"Kat," I say. I'm on my hands and knees, trying to make eye contact with her. "You are NOT dying. Definitely not." I think fast. "I have to go to the drugstore and get you something, something to soak up the blood." I can't bring myself to say tampons or pads. They sound like dirty words. "It's completely normal," I tell her, trying to recall what they told us in family life class. I hadn't paid much attention during the girl stuff, thinking, of course, that I didn't really need to know about it. But how could I have forgotten about Kat? I guess I never pictured her growing up.

"You stay right here." I point at the floor, which I realize is kind of stupid. Why should she stay on the bathroom floor?

She nods, drops her face into her knees and sobs again.

Now that I know the problem is not life threatening, I realize there is something else I can add to my mental list. Dramatics. Kat's getting real good at dramatics. Oh yeah. And periods. I can add that too. Shit.

I pull on some clothes, grab my wallet and jog down the street. Fortunately there is a convenience store nearby.

Now, I'm not stupid. I've seen enough TV commercials to know exactly what to buy. Something
with wings. Something with maximum absorbency
but minimum bulkiness. Something ultra-thin and
disposable. But when I find the aisle I'm looking for
and see the display, I'm stunned. Christ! There must
be thirty different brands and types! What does an
eleven-year-old girl who is just starting need? Overnighters? Light days? Medium protection? Heavy
protection? Extra long? Extra narrow? All of the
above? There are even thong-shaped ones!

"Can I help you?"

I find myself looking straight into the eyes of a
young salesgirl. She's wearing a geeky vest, which I
guess is supposed to be a uniform. A badge pinned to
her chest proves she really does work here. I stare at
the badge too long, trying to avoid her eyes. "Uh, no,"
I say. "Just looking." Jeez. I'm so pathetic.

"Okay," she says, giving me the once-over. "Just let me
know if you need some," she pauses, "help." She glances at
the display, looks at me once more and then turns abruptly
and sashays down the aisle. Oh yeah. Just what I need
right now. A smart-ass salesgirl who thinks she's hot.

I can't do this. The display is totally overwhelming
and I'm too embarrassed to stand around reading each
package, trying to figure out which brand Kat needs. I
leave the store and drop onto a bus-stop bench. I have
to help Kat. What can I do?

I decide to call Mrs. K. She'll help me. There's a pay
phone right outside the store.

Mrs. K picks up after one ring. "Hello?"

"Mrs. Kippenstein, it's me, Darcy."

"Darcy." She sounds alarmed. "Is everything okay? Aren't you in school today?"

"Yeah, everything's okay, sort of, but no, I'm not in school. Kat woke up with this problem and…"

"What's the problem?"

I swallow hard and then let it fly. "She's bleeding. I think she's got her first…period. I went to the store to get her, you know, stuff, but I didn't know what to buy."

"No, why would you?" she laughs a little, but she sounds about as uncomfortable as I feel. "Is she at home?"

"Yeah."

"Listen," she says in a take-charge voice. "I'll pick up what she needs and be at your house in about half an hour. How does that sound?"

"That'd be great. Thanks, Mrs. Kippenstein."

"You're welcome. And tell her everything is okay. It's perfectly normal."

"I did. But she's pretty upset."

There's a pause. "She does know what it's all about, doesn't she?"

"I don't know." I didn't. "I assume so."

Another pause. "My God, maybe nobody has ever told her!"

I suddenly feel extremely negligent. Is that why she was so hysterical?

"Tell her I'm on my way." She hangs up. So do I.

I walk home slowly, disturbed by what has happened. Things are changing way too fast. Something tells me that the universe is not as erratic and random as I've always assumed, or wanted to assume. First I find out that Mom might be getting out of jail. Then Dad says Kat needs her mom. I disagree, but two days later she gets her period and I can't even help her. She does need her mom. Or a mom. A big brother is just not good enough. If her starting her period today is not some kind of wake-up call for me, what is?

MRS. K COMES into the kitchen, where I'm putting together a Winnie-the-Pooh puzzle with Sammy. "She's never even heard of menstruation," Mrs. K says, very clinically.

"Really?" I guide Sammy's hand to the hole in the puzzle where the piece she is clutching fits in. "Don't all schools go over that stuff in family life class?"

She shakes her head. "Maybe not at her school. Or maybe she was away that day. I dunno." She sighs and slumps into a chair. "She's fallen through the cracks somehow. The poor wee thing is pretty traumatized." I decide to strike dramatics off my list. Poor kid. She probably did think she was dying.

"Anyway, she has plenty of…of supplies to get her through this month and next, although at her age it might be six months before she gets it again. I think your dad should buy her a book about puberty."

I guess my expression painted a pretty clear picture of the possibility of that ever happening.

"Okay, how about I find one at the library for her," Mrs. K suggests.

"That would be great, thanks."

"You're welcome. And Darcy, I'm glad you called me this morning. It was the right thing to do."

"I'm just glad you were home." That is the understatement of the century.

"I'll call work and say I can't make it today," she says, "so you and Kat can stay home."

That reminds me. "Actually, my dad has planned something for us a week from Wednesday night, so we can't baby-sit then. Maybe we should come tonight, seeing as…"

"Don't worry about it, Darcy," she says. "I'll make other arrangements, both for tonight and next Wednesday night. My brother and his wife are always happy to take her."

I wonder if this is the beginning of the end of my baby-sitting job.

Mrs. K gets up and signs for Sammy to put her coat on, but Sam bursts into tears instead. It seems she's having way too much fun with "her" Darcy. I hope Mrs. K is taking notes. I lean over and tell her, with my hands, that I will see her tomorrow. She gives me a big hug—I can't believe such a small kid can hug so hard—and I wave to her as she leaves. Watching them get into Mrs. K's car, I wish that Kat was still such a little girl. I wish I were still a little boy. We'd had our own baby-sitter then, one who could sign with Kat and who did puzzles with me. Someone else to be responsible.

I find Kat sitting on her bed, holding the same stuffed animal that she'd been hugging on Saturday night. "You okay?" I ask.

She nods. Her eyes are still puffy and sore, but I detect something else in them too. "Mrs. K says I'm a woman now," she tells me with her hands. The corner of her mouth twitches and I know she's trying not to smile.

"That just shows how well she doesn't know you," I sign.

She sticks her tongue out at me.

"I didn't realize that no one had ever explained that stuff to you."

She shakes her head and continues with her hands. "Now I get what those ads on TV are about. When I was little I thought those things were something you ate."

I can't help but laugh. She smiles, remembering.

"When I finally realized they weren't food, I couldn't figure out what they were for."

You miss a lot when you're a deaf kid in a hearing world.

"So, what do you want to do with the rest of our day? We're not baby-sitting tonight."

She just shrugs.

"Why don't we catch a bus and go to the Wildlife Refuge Center. It won't be nearly so crowded on a weekday."

Her eyes light up. There's nothing she likes better than being around animals.

"I'll phone your school and tell them you're home sick today."

WHEN SHE COMES into the kitchen she's wearing her just-like-new jeans and sweater. "Can you see anything?" she asks.

I guess I must look confused, because she suddenly gets agitated. "Down there," she signs, without telling me where "there" is.

Then I get it. I guess I can be a little thick sometimes, especially when it comes to girl stuff. I glance "down there" and then force myself to meet her eyes. "Not at all," my hands assure her.

"How about at the back?" She turns around, pauses and then turns back to face me again.

I shake my head.

She scowls. "It feels like wearing diapers."

I nod, sympathetically, but inside I feel a rage welling up. No eleven-year-old girl should have to talk to her fifteen-year-old brother about these things. More importantly, no big brother should have to hear them. Kat needs a mom, an aunt, a sister, anybody female.

"Darcy?" Kat asks, snapping me out of my black thoughts. "I need a purse." She spells out the word "purse" with her fingers. "To carry stuff in. Do you think we could stop at the mall on the way there?"

I'm not so stupid that I have to ask her what the stuff is that she has to carry in the purse. I just nod yes and grab my coat from the closet.

But I feel that murderous gene rearing its ugly head again.

"WE MISSED YOU yesterday, Darcy. Everything okay?"

The Rose has her doe eyes resting on me again. I glance at her, then look back at my page. I have to fight the urge to say something flippant like, oh yeah, I had a great day scrubbing bloodstains out of my little sister's sheets, but with a deep sigh I control myself and resort to the usual, "Everything's fine."

"That's good." I know she's nodding, trying to force me to look at her again.

I don't. Instead I get busy copying today's quote from the board.

People are lonely because they build walls instead of bridges. —Joseph F. Newton

The Rose must think we're stupid or something. And sometimes I wonder, suspiciously, if she chooses these sayings with me in mind, but then I realize how lame that is. I'm as important to The Rose as a single soggy seed in a forest.

As usual, I refuse to give her what she wants.

In this quote Joseph F. (I wonder what the F stands for. Fred? Freak? Why not just write out the whole name?) Newton is telling us that it is better to be an engineer than a masonry-type person. This is because engineers build bridges, and according to Joe F., engineers are not as lonely as the wall builders. Just another reason to get a good education, I guess.

I know there are a few gigantic holes in my argument, but I can always hope that The Rose will appreciate my creativity. No doubt everyone else gave her the obvious response.

On the break I plug in another CD. Snapping the headphones on, I close my eyes and lose myself in the music. I'm really getting into it when I feel a presence beside me. I open my eyes and find Gem, the girl who sits beside me in class, standing at my elbow. I pull off my headphones. "What?"

"Nothing. Just wondering what you're listening to."

"None of your business."

"You're right." She blows a gum bubble and then sucks it back in with a snap. "Mind if I sit here?" she asks, pulling out the chair beside mine.

"I don't own it," I say, but glance pointedly around the library, taking in all the empty chairs farther away, hoping she gets the hint.

She doesn't, but then I really didn't expect her to.

"How come you're not out smoking?" I ask.

"Gave it up," she says. "My boyfriend says I don't taste so good when he kisses me."

"I guess not."

"How 'bout you?"

"I never started."

"Oh, that's right. I bet your girlfriend loves kissing you."

"I don't have a girlfriend."

"Really?" she asks, pretending to look me over. "I'm surprised." She snaps another bubble and then says, "You never look at girls so I figured you were taken."

"You figured wrong." I press the stop button on my Discman. A good song is probably playing and I'm missing it.

"Truth is," she says, averting her eyes, "I don't have a boyfriend either. But when I do find the right one, I don't want to have nicotine breath. My dad smoked and when he used to kiss me goodnight, I'd just about gag."

I wonder if Gem's parents knew she was going to have such amazing eyes when they named her. They're the translucent aqua of a precious stone, and they change color depending on the light. You'd expect brown eyes with her dark skin and hair, so it's always a shock when she looks directly at you, which she's doing now. I look away quickly. "What do you want, Gem?" I ask. I'm not stupid enough to believe this is just a social call.

"What makes you think I want something?" she asks. "Can't we just have a conversation?"

"Maybe another time," I say. "I was enjoying a CD."

"Suit yourself," she says, reaching into her bag and pulling out her own Discman. But just before I can push the play button on my machine she asks, "You're not gay, are you?"

I pull my headphones off and look at her again. "Is that what they're saying about me now?"

"It's just speculation."

"And were you sent here to find out for sure?"

"No!" Her reaction convinces me that she's telling the truth. "I don't really care one way or the other," she says. "But it is odd when a guy takes no notice of girls." She shrugs. "You can be AC/DC for all I care. I was just wondering, that's all." She puts on her headphones and presses play.

I press play too, but I don't hear the music. I'm thinking about what she's just said. I know I'm not into guys. At all. There's no question about that. But she's right. I'm not particularly into girls either. I've just always figured I didn't need the hassle.

GEM FOLLOWS ME into the library again at lunchtime. "Are you my new best friend or something?" I ask her.

She looks at me, kind of hurt like. "Have you got a problem with me hangin' out with you?" she asks.

"Not really," I say. "It's just that I'm wondering why the sudden interest."

She studies me. "I'm just trying to build one of those bridges, Darcy, but you keep putting up walls."

Oh God. She's taken The Rose's quote to heart. I feel my stomach give a little twist. "Did I let on that I was lonely?" I ask her. "Because if I did, I'm sorry. But I'm absolutely not. I'm not today. I won't be tomorrow, and I wasn't yesterday. If that's not clear enough for you…"

She doesn't say anything. She doesn't have to. The look on her face shows she understands perfectly. With a flash of her eyes she does an about-turn and leaves the room.

Breathing hard, I grab a CD off the rack without even looking at the title and plug it in. The music is soft and mellow. I close my eyes and sink back into my chair. I feel my breathing begin to slow, even though my eyes still burn with unwanted tears. Concentrating

on the song, I allow myself to be seduced by its sooth-
ing rhythms. I feel myself escaping, being drawn back
to the safe place, the place where no one can find me.
I'm not afraid of being alone there. No one can hurt
me when I'm alone. No one but myself. I rub the new
welts on my arm.

Five

The pendulum of Kat's moods appears to be stuck on the side labeled Bad. She's always cranky now, and no amount of clowning on my part cheers her up. In fact, if I didn't know better, I'd say she's avoiding me. I've had to start setting an alarm clock at night because she no longer wakes up on her own in the morning. She only picks at her food and she spends a lot of time in her room just sitting at her desk. She's so miserable that even Dad notices.

"Is she okay?" he asks. Kat and I have just returned from baby-sitting and she heads straight to her room.

"I don't know." I don't. But I decide to try my hand at passing blame. "Could have something to do with those newspaper articles you handed her on Sunday."

I won't swear to it, but I think I see a trace of remorse flicker across his face.

IT TURNS OUT I did a better job of tapping into Dad's guilty conscience than I meant to.

A car sporting a *Working Dogs Association* bumper sticker is parked right outside our townhouse when we get home from baby-sitting on Thursday night. I spot it from half a block away. So does Kat. Her sharp eyes don't miss a thing. She glances at me. "Do you think?" she asks, incredulously.

I shake my head. "No, Kat," I sign. "Don't go there. Dad's not going to change his mind now." Especially now, seeing as he's planning to get rid of her.

But I guess she doesn't believe me. She jogs up the stairs and into the house. I follow quietly behind, feeling slightly sick and wondering what Dad could possibly be scheming now.

We find him sitting in the living room with the lady who—no doubt—owns the car. At her side is a golden retriever, its silky head cocked as it watches us enter. It doesn't move, even though you can see by the ears that tilt forward and by the eager, copper-colored eyes that it wants to come over and give us a good sniffing.

"Darcy, Kat," says Dad, "this is Eileen Gilbert. She trains dogs to work with people who have…" he pauses, looking for the correct word, "physical challenges." Dad smiles, proud of himself for remembering the term. I have to restrain myself from rolling my eyes. He's such a big fat fake.

"Hello, Kat. Darcy," Eileen signs, to her credit. "This is Star, one of the dogs I've been training."

The dog watches her hands as if it, too, knows sign language. Eileen pats its head.

"Why are you here?" I figure there's no point beating about the bush. This is clearly not someone who would date Dad, and besides, Dad doesn't bring his girlfriends home to meet the kids.

"Your dad invited me, Darcy," she answers, kindly.

I turn to him. "Dad?"

He at least has the sense to look a little embarrassed. "Your sister's been whining about getting one of these dogs for months," he says, then turns to Eileen. "She saw a special on TV about a dog who could predict when his epileptic owner was about to have a seizure. Supposedly this dog could then protect her from hurting herself." He glances skeptically at Star, then back to Eileen. "Since then she hasn't shut up about getting her own." He tries to look fondly at Kat, then shakes his head, as if he always gives in to her whims. He must have forgotten that Kat can't whine, she rarely talks and when she does, he doesn't understand her anyway.

Eileen must have missed those minor points too. She smiles and nods at Kat, her hand still on the dog's head.

"But, Dad," I remind him, trying hard not to sound sarcastic. Unfortunately, I don't think I'm up for the challenge. "You always said, 'No. No way. Not in my lifetime,' or words to that effect." I think I've done a pretty good imitation of his tone. Nasty is easy to imitate.

Dad glances quickly at Eileen, but turns back to me. His eyes meet mine, and he gives me the look, the one telling me I've crossed the line. His words, though, say something quite different. "Everyone's allowed to change their mind, now, aren't they, Darcy?"

I don't answer. I don't have to because Kat is changing the subject by signing to Eileen, asking if she can pat the dog. I can see from the look on her face that she's past being simply hopeful. She's smitten.

Eileen tells Kat that she is welcome to pat the dog, so Kat kneels down, offers a hand to be sniffed and then, after stroking its head a few times, puts her arms around its neck in a big hug. The dog responds by licking her ears and neck. It's really quite pathetic.

"Star likes you," Eileen signs. "Look at the way her tail is thumping."

Kat grins and continues stroking the dog. They are gazing at each other like reunited lovers.

I have to leave the room. It's too much.

LATER, WHEN I HEAR Eileen's car starting up, I come out of my bedroom.

"What the hell is your problem!" Dad bellows before I can say a thing.

I tell Kat to go to bed and then follow Dad back into the living room where he flops into the armchair, but Kat's no dummy and she isn't going to be left out of this conversation. Dad's up to something and she wants to know what it is. She stands in the living room doorway.

"Ask him if we're getting a dog," she signs at me, desperately. "Tell him I want Star."

"You go to bed and I'll talk to him," I say with my hands. "I'll find out what's going on and then I'll come and tell you."

She thinks about this, meets Dad's eyes and then looks back at me. The next thing I know she is bent over Dad, giving him a hug. "Thanks, Dad!" she says, almost clearly. Then she rushes out of the room.

Kat has a few tricks up her own sleeve.

I turn to Dad.

"What did she just say to you?" he asks. It irks him that he can't understand us, but not enough, I guess, to actually learn to sign himself. He usually resorts to pen and paper when he has something he has to say and I'm not handy. But I can see that the hug has caught him off guard. He actually looks a little shaken.

"She said to tell you she wants Star."

"That was obvious."

"What are you up to, Dad? Are you really planning to get her a dog?"

"I'm considering it," he says, reaching into his pocket for his cigarettes. "Find me some matches, will you, son?"

Son? What's going on here? I study him for a moment, can't get an accurate reading on his scheming and so go to the kitchen to look for matches and an ashtray. As I pass the telephone I notice the answering machine light flashing. I hit the play button and then rummage through a drawer full of junk. A deep voice fills the room. "Hello. This is Michael Zabonosky from the *Daily*, just calling to confirm our interview scheduled for next Wednesday evening. We look forward to meeting all of you then." There is an emphasis on "all of you."

Feeling the blood drain from my head, I return to the living room, without matches. "You have no intention of getting her a dog."

"Why do you say that?" Dad's found his lighter while I was in the kitchen. He probably knew that he had it all along. He puts the flame to the tip of his cigarette.

"You just want her to think you are so she'll tell the newspaper people that. You want to convince them that you've been a great daddy."

He takes a long drag on the cigarette. "When did you become so cynical, Darcy?"

"You're not going to get away with it, Dad. I won't let you get her hopes up and then break her heart."

"I'm gonna get her a dog."

I just stare at him. He really must be feeling guilty about the other night.

"It will be your mother's problem in no time."

So we're back to that. "Have you ever thought that our mother might not want Kat? She did try to kill her, in case you've forgotten, and I really don't think the authorities are going to let her have Kat back."

"In the eyes of the law, Darcy, your mother will have served her time, and she's entitled to a fresh start."

"But what if she doesn't want Kat?" I'm having trouble keeping my voice steady.

"She does. She's made it clear. She's even taken American Sign Language instruction in prison. She's fully prepared to resume her parental responsibilities."

The smug expression on his face is too much.

"You're going to regret this, Dad." Furious, I turn to leave the room.

"Is that a threat, Darcy?" His tone has changed. The taunting bully is back.

"No, it's not. It's a statement."

I FIND KAT in bed, the glare of the bare overhead bulb casting a harsh light through the room. She springs to a sitting position. "Well?"

"Do you want the good news or the bad news first?"

"Darcy," she says, ticked off. "Do I get a dog or not?"

I sit on her bed and study her. Her anxious face turns my hardened heart to mush. "Yeah, he's going to find you a dog, but…"

I don't get a chance to finish the sentence. Her arms are around my neck and she is squeezing so hard I'm afraid I'm being strangled.

I peel her off. "He's only doing it for show, Kat, to make everyone in town think he's such a great daddy. I think he's actually feeling guilty about being a lousy parent. But he intends for you to go live with our mom, and who knows if she'll be willing to keep a dog."

Kat studies me. "I don't care why he's doing it," she signs. "I just want a dog. And if she wants me, she'll have to take the dog too." She folds her arms across her chest.

I don't even want to think about this stuff. "Go to sleep, Kat. I'll see you in the morning."

I have to blink back the tears. Things are definitely not going to work out the way she thinks.

I turn, but before I can leave the room she calls my name.

"What?"

The joy has left her eyes, and now she looks concerned.

"Let me see your arm," she signs.

There she goes again. That uncanny way of knowing, often before I do, when I have to use the knife.

"My arm is none of your business," I sign back and leave the room. She doesn't follow.

THE INTERVIEW WITH the two guys from the *Daily* goes pretty much the way Dad orchestrated it. Kat is still flying high in anticipation of a dog, so I'm sure she comes across as a happy, well-adjusted kid. I'm my usual insolent self, but they probably put that down to my age. Dad sits in his armchair with this aren't-I-one-heck-of-a-wonderful-guy expression on his face, calling me "son" and telling tales of what a stupendous job he's done of raising his kids, all on his own. Forgotten, it seems, is that fact that he can't communicate with his daughter. Perhaps I should roll up my sleeve.

When they ask him what he'll do when our mom gets out of jail and wants custody of us, he slumps down and pretends to struggle with the question.

"It'll be really tough," he says, finally, "but in all fairness, I believe I should allow Sherri her share of time with them. I don't believe she's a bad person. I think the attempted murder was a one-time act of desperation, possibly triggered by drugs, alcohol and depression." Dad glances at the tape recorder sitting on the coffee table in front of him, assuring himself that all this B.S. is being recorded. I have to give the guy credit; I didn't know he was such a good actor. He recites the memorized lines flawlessly.

"I understand from the authorities," he continues, "that she's received counseling for her addictions, and she's even completed her high school diploma. That sounds to me like she's a woman who's no longer a threat to society or her children, and it's only fair to give her a second chance."

It's enough to make you puke, but just when I'm feeling completely defeated, ready to admit that Dad has won this particular battle, Kat pulls a fast one on him.

The two news guys have shut off the recorder and are packing up their things. Kat is watching them intently. She turns to me and signs rapidly. "Ask them if they like dogs," she says.

I don't know what she's up to, but I ask anyway.

The guy packing up the camera smiles and nods at Kat. I can see he thinks she's adorable.

"Now ask him if he'd like to come and meet my dog when I get him."

I can't help but laugh at her cunning, but of course the news guy just thinks I'm laughing at how cute she is.

He falls right into her trap. "Tell her I'd love to," he says after I extend the invitation. "And why don't you ask her if she'd mind us doing a follow-up story about her and her dog. It would be interesting to see how they are getting on, and if the dog really can be trained to protect her during seizures."

I don't even have to translate. Kat gets the general gist just by reading his lips. She grins, triumphant. Now Dad *has* to get her a dog.

THE HEADLINE IN the paper the following morning takes me by surprise once again. **Sherri Murphy Gets Full Parole** it says in mile-high letters on the front page. I didn't realize it was going to happen so soon.

When I arrive at school I see a small throng of adults milling around the door. They're carrying cameras, microphones and notepads.

"There he is!" a voice declares, and before I know it I'm surrounded. People are yelling questions into my face and cameras are flashing.

I shove my way through, planting my elbow into soft flesh whenever I can. I find Mr. Bryson trying to reach me from the other side. He grabs my arm and pulls me toward the school. The door is opened by someone watching from inside, and Mr. Bryson shoves me in before turning and facing the media people. I can hear him ordering them off the school grounds.

Ms. LaRose is right there, her arm wrapped protectively about my shoulder. There's that scent again, that soft, comforting fragrance. I'd like to bury my face in her chest, inhale her perfume...

"I have to find out if Kat is okay!" I can't believe I forgot about her, even momentarily. "I need to phone her school."

She nods and steers me into the school office. I know the number and punch it in quickly, trying to ignore the fact that my hand is shaking.

"Sunshine School for the Deaf."

"This is Darcy Fraser," I tell the female voice. "I'm wondering if my sister is okay. There's people here with cameras and..."

"Oh, hi, Darcy," she says, sighing loudly. "There was a small crowd of reporters here too, waiting for her bus, but we were able to get her safely into the school."

That didn't make me feel much better. "Is she okay? Did it scare her?"

"She's okay." There was a pause. "What shall we do about after school?"

She's got me there. Usually we meet at the Kippensteins'.

"Should I call your father and have him pick her up?" she asks.

"I guess you could try. You'll have to leave a message with his dispatcher."

"What about you?"

Good question. "Tell him to pick me up too."

"Okay, I'll do that," she says calmly. She'd make a good 9-1-1 operator. "And I'll leave a message confirming it for you at your school. Okay?"

"Yeah." The sickening truth is dawning on me. Dad's gonna love this attention. He'll be only too happy to pick us up today.

When I hang up the phone I realize Ms. LaRose is still standing there. We stare at each other. "Do you want to talk about it?" she asks softly.

I long to say yes. Yes. Yes. Yes.

"No. I'm fine."

She nods, and we walk down to our classroom together.

DAD'S OUTSIDE, TALKING to the reporters, when school gets out. Kat has herself locked in the car. I grit my teeth and push my way past them. Kat lets me in and we wait for Dad, who is blathering away, totally enjoying himself.

"You okay?" I ask her.

She just nods and turns to look out the window.

I poke her arm to get her attention. "Do you know why they're here?" I ask.

She nods again.

I study her serious face. There's no sign of the coy little girl who charmed the newspaper reporters last night.

That mood pendulum, which had so briefly become unstuck, has now swung back to where it was sitting last week.

WHEN THE MEDIA get what they want or, more likely, realize what an ass Dad is, they begin to disperse, but not before pointing their cameras at the car, trying to take our picture through the glass. I cover my face with my hands. I don't know what Kat does.

"Just drop us off at the Kippensteins'," I tell Dad when he finally gets in the car.

"This was nothing," he says, gesturing at the dispersing crowd and ignoring my request. He's pumped, more excited than I've ever seen him. "You should have seen the crowd outside the prison today."

"You saw it?"

"I saw it on the noon news."

"You were watching TV at noon?"

"I stopped by Rusty's for lunch."

Rusty's is a pub. I decide not to ask why he would go to a pub for lunch, but there has been something else I've wanted to ask. "Where's she going to live?"

"Her parole officer has found an apartment for her." He laughs. "I'm betting he didn't tell the landlord who was moving in."

"Will she be safe?" Not that I really care.

"These people are full of hot air. Of course she'll be safe."

I glance at Kat. She's still staring out the window. "What makes you think Kat will be safe if she goes back to her?"

"No one has a problem with Kat." Dad blasts his horn at someone making a left turn in front of him.

"In fact," he says, "Kat's presence just might keep your mom safe."

"Why wouldn't Mom move to another town?"

He glances at me. "Good question, Darcy. And she might, depending on what you decide to do."

"Me?"

"Yeah, you."

"What have I got to do with it?"

"If you go live with her, she'll be able to leave."

"Huh?"

"I told her I didn't think she should separate you and Kat. That you're pretty close."

"You've been talking to her?"

"We've had a couple of meetings."

This really surprises me. "You didn't think I'd like to know this?"

"Darcy, you've made it quite clear that your mother is not someone you want to talk about. Or live with." Dad has pulled into the Kippensteins' driveway.

"So you told her we're pretty close and shouldn't be separated?"

"That's right."

There's something wrong with this picture. "Why would you do that?"

"It's true, isn't it?"

"Yeah, but..."

"And if we're both in the same town, you'll be able to see your sister."

"And if she moves away..."

"Then Kat might refuse to go."

Now I get it. He's not going to take a chance that he gets stuck with Kat one day longer than he has to.

I see that the Kippensteins' front door is open and Sammy is standing there, waiting for us. Kat climbs out of the car and is greeted with a hug. I'm feeling like there must be something else I need to say to Dad, but my mind is blank. Things are happening way too fast.

MY DREAM IS interrupted by a cold hand on my shoulder. I don't want to wake up. I'm in a safe, warm place that smells like roses...

"Darcy," Kat says.

I force my eyes open and see her standing ghostlike beside my bed.

"Can I sleep with you?"

This is a first. In the past she just climbed in.

I pull back the blankets and move over. Way over. She climbs in but stays close to the edge. She turns so her back is to me. Even from a few inches away I can sense the tension in her body as she clings to the edge of the bed.

I remember how Kat used to press her cold little body up against mine, pop her thumb in her mouth and we'd fall asleep, like a couple of kittens snoozing in a wicker basket.

I roll over so my back is to her. I feel like a shit.

SHE'S GONE WHEN I wake up. I find her in the kitchen eating cereal. "Are you okay?" I ask.

"Yeah." There are black smudges under her eyes.

I pour myself a bowl of cereal and join her at the table.

"I want to meet her," she signs. It comes out of nowhere.

"Our mom?"

"Yeah."

"I don't think you have much choice about that."

"I know. I just want you to know I'm okay with it."

"You're not mad at her?"

She shakes her head, looking thoughtful. "I don't remember anything. It's different for you. You have bad memories."

We go back to eating.

"I just want a mom." She brushes a tear off her cheek.

My heart aches for her. "I'm afraid you're going to be disappointed," I sign. "She hasn't been a model parent so far."

Kat shrugs. "I was afraid you'd be mad at me."

"For what?"

"For wanting to see her."

"Oh, Kat."

"I want to give her a chance."

"Okay."

"But I don't want to let you down."

"How would you be letting me down?"

"I know you hate her, so I feel like I'm supposed to hate her too."

I really am a shit.

On Friday night we spot Eileen Gilbert's car parked outside again. Kat immediately breaks into a sprint, covering the last half of the block in seconds. By the time I arrive in the living room, Kat is on the floor stroking Star, and Dad and Eileen are sitting at the table, reading over some official-looking documents.

"I get to keep her all weekend!" Kat signs to me.

"Yeah?" She should tell someone who cares.

Eileen comes back to the living room and greets me. "Your dad tells me that he's ready to give dog owner-ship a try," she says. "Star is a well-mannered, gentle dog who responds to a lot of sign language already. She didn't quite make it as a guide dog, but I think she'd be a really good pet for your sister. And it may turn out that she can protect Kat during a seizure."

I nod, not knowing what to say.

"I'll be back to pick her up on Sunday afternoon. We'll talk about how the weekend went then." She pats Star one last time and then quietly slips out the door.

Dad and I stand in the kitchen, looking down on Kat and Star. She looks up at us with tears in her eyes. "Thanks, Dad," she says.

He glances quickly at me before turning back to her. He clears his throat. "You're welcome," he says.

"Let's take her for a walk, Darcy," Kat suggests with her hands.

"You go ahead. I'm feeling a little lazy right now." That's a lie. I am feeling something, but I'm not sure what it is.

"You sure?" she asks.

"Yeah."

Kat puts Star on her leash, tucks a plastic bag in her pocket as Eileen instructed and heads out the door. I watch them from the living room window. Star trots along at Kat's side, looking up at her now and then. Kat's so happy she's practically dancing down the sidewalk.

"She is kinda cute, isn't she," Dad says, coming up beside me.

I look at him. "Who? The dog?"

He laughs. "Yeah, she's okay for a dog. But I meant Kat."

I don't say anything. It's too bizarre. Dad is finally taking notice of his daughter just before he plans to pack her up and ship her off.

I FIND STAR lying right beside Kat's bed when I go in to say good night. She scrambles up to greet me when I come into the room.

"Lie down," I order.

Star looks hurt but pads back to her place beside Kat.

"Don't you just love her?" Kat asks, unaware of how sharply I just spoke.

"Oh, yeah," I answer. "I just love her to pieces."

Kat knows from the expression on my face that I'm not serious. "You will, Darcy. Once you get used to her."

Yeah right, I think. Like that's going to happen.

KAT BURSTS INTO tears when she sees Eileen pulling up to our house on Sunday afternoon. She has spent every waking moment of the weekend with Star, and I swear she's taught that dog more sign language than you'd think was possible.

Dad lets Eileen into the house. Eileen's glance takes in Kat, who is now sobbing uncontrollably, and then Dad, who just shrugs. "She doesn't want you to take Star back," he says.

"Oh," she says. "They must be getting along."

"That they are," Dad agrees.

"We can extend the trial period if you like," she says to my dad.

"I think we're going to have to," he says, turning his back to Kat. "But I must tell you, Eileen. Kat is probably moving back in with her mother soon. I hope that won't change anything."

"Have you asked her mother if she's willing to take a dog?"

"No," Dad admits. He pauses, and in that moment I see an odd expression cross his face, as if he's just remembered something relevant. He thinks about it, but says only, "I doubt it'll be a problem."

Eileen looks skeptical. "If she's going back to her mother, why did you choose now to get her a dog?" I notice a hint of irritation in her voice. "I have the dog's welfare to consider too, and I wasn't anticipating another move for her so soon."

"The timing isn't perfect, I know," he says. "It's just the way it worked out. And besides," he adds, "maybe the dog will help Kat make the transition better.

Eileen turns to face Kat and Star again. "Hi, Star," she says.

Star's tail thumps on the floor but she doesn't leave Kat's side.

"Come, Star," she signs.

With an anxious look at the sobbing Kat, Star pads across the floor to Eileen's side. "Good girl," she says. She strokes the dog and talks quietly to her. Eventually she speaks to Dad again. "I can see that Star has adapted well to Kat," she says. "I'll leave her, if you like, and we'll just keep our fingers crossed that the move to Kat's mom's goes smoothly. I won't finalize the adoption until we see how it works out."

Dad nods. "Thank you. I'm sure everything will work out fine, but that's probably a good plan."

Eileen signs to Kat. "Would you like to keep her a little longer?" she asks.

Kat nods and wipes her nose with the back of her hand. "How long?"

"We're not sure yet. But for a while."

Kat jumps up and scampers across the room to hug Eileen. Then she hugs Star again. Star's tail thumps and she barks once.

That ugly feeling in the pit of my stomach has returned and I have to leave the room. I'm sure Kat doesn't even notice.

Six

Star's arrival has wreaked havoc with our perfectly ordered routine. Now that Kat has to walk and feed her in the morning, she no longer has time to make me breakfast or pack me a lunch. In the commotion this morning, Kat almost forgot to take her medication—despite reminders from me—and she became a blubbering idiot when it was time to say goodbye to the dog and get on the bus.

I am all but forgotten.

To make matters worse, the front page of today's paper features Mom's release from prison. Dad was right. In the picture, the gathered mob looks angry, and Mom looks scared to death. Serves her right.

Turning the page I find myself staring into my own eyes. Talk about a vacant expression. Beside me in the picture is my father, his phony-ass arm draped across my shoulder, and Kat is leaning against me on the other side. The story doesn't say much, except for some drivel about how forgiving and gracious we all are about Mom's release. No doubt they'd been hoping to run a scandalous story featuring an over-protective, loving father and his fearful, distrusting children, all of whom are appalled that the mother is being given parole. I bet we were a big disappointment. Maybe I should have spoken up. Exposing some of our secrets might have put us on the front page, right there beside Mom. As it is, Ms. Wetzell's fireworks seem to be fizzling out.

Just as I'm about to leave—lunchless—I notice Star and her sad brown eyes staring at me from the doorway to Kat's bedroom. I have to be careful. This is one cagey dog. She figures if she's patient long enough, and good enough, and pretty enough, I'll eventually give in and love her. I can't let that happen. I turn and go out the door without a word.

Unfortunately, I have to come home and collect her after school. Kat has permission from Mrs. K to bring her baby-sitting with us, and it's up to me to come home and fetch her before heading over there.

She greets me warily, tail wagging, but not too enthusiastically. I put on her leash and we begin the six-block walk.

It is an unnerving experience.

Complete strangers feel that having a pretty dog at your side is an open invitation for interaction, to pat it and to tell you all about their dog or their neighbor's dog or their great aunt's dog. Kids are the worst. They're all over Star, mauling her and asking me dumb questions. What kind of dog is she? How old is she? Is she a girl dog or a boy dog?

I'm beginning to think I may never get to Sammy's.

Then, just when I've unraveled myself from the last one and Sammy's driveway is almost in sight, a car pulls up to the curb and Gem jumps out of the passenger seat.

"Darcy! I didn't know you had a golden retriever," she squeals. She puts her hand out to let Star sniff her and then gives the dog's back a good hard thumping. Star seems to enjoy it. Gem must know something about dogs. I glance into the car and meet the eyes of the driver. He looks unimpressed.

"She's not mine," I tell her. "She's my little sister's, at least for now."

"For now?"

"We've got her on a trial basis, to see if it works out."

"Hmm." Now Gem has one of Star's ears in each hand and is gently massaging them. The skin on the back of her hands is the color of milk chocolate. Her nails are painted pale pink. "She's a real beauty."

I have nothing to say to that. I glance again at the driver of the car. He's glaring back at me. "I thought you didn't have a boyfriend," I say.

"I don't," Gem says. She glances at the driver too. "That's just my brother."

"Oh." Why am I relieved to hear that?

"I gotta go," I say, finally dragging my eyes away from her hands. For a moment I find myself wishing I were Star, or at least Star's ears. What has come over me? I'm getting soft. "I'm late for work."

She leans over and kisses the top of the dog's head. Yuck. And she's worried about having nicotine breath?

"See you tomorrow," she says before hopping back into her brother's car.

I FIND KAT and Sammy waiting in the front yard for us. With delighted squeals they race over and greet Star. I may as well be invisible. Mrs. K comes out of the house and greets the dog too. Maybe I'll just leave and let Star baby-sit.

"Hi, Darcy," Mrs. K says, finally. "I saw your picture in the paper today."

"Oh, yeah."

She gives me a look I can't read. "Everything all right?" she asks.

"Yep."

"Good," she says, nodding. "And Kat? She's dealing with everything okay?"

I'm not quite sure what she's referring to, but it doesn't really matter. "Yeah, Star's taken her mind off everything else."

"That's good."

I have to agree with that.

"I have to run," she says. "I left a note on the counter for you." She turns to leave.

"Okay."

"Oh." She swings back around to face me. "I also mentioned in the note that Geoff and I have both decided to take next week off, to spend it with Sammy."

"Oh. Okay." Geoff is Sammy's dad.

"I'm sorry about the short notice, Darcy, but," she frowns, "we're a little concerned about her."

"You are?"

"Yeah, we've noticed that she just hasn't been herself. We're hoping that she just needs a little more of our attention."

Actually, I've noticed that Sammy's been acting kind of strange too. She's been more clingy than ever, but then lashes out at the strangest things. "Okay. No problem."

"Thanks, Darcy. I appreciate that. And a week off will be like a little holiday for you, won't it? Maybe you can hang out with your friends, play some sports or something."

Shows how well she knows me. I smile politely and nod.

"All right then, I'm gone," she says. Sammy is chasing Star, who seems to understand the game of tag perfectly. Mrs. K hugs Sam, who doesn't hug back or become anxious because she's too busy struggling to be set loose. Star is way more interesting than her mother at this moment. Or me.

How quickly I've been replaced.

MS. WETZELL CALLS me into her office.

"How's it going, Darcy?" she asks.

"Fine."

"Your mom is out of prison now."

"That's what I hear."

"And you survived the media frenzy."

"So far so good."

"I wonder how your mom is faring. She'll be recognized wherever she goes. It won't be easy."

"That's not my problem."

She sighs. "I got a call from your sister's school this morning. It's a message for you. Apparently your dad called them to say he's decided to pick Kat up early and take her over to see your mom."

"He has? Why didn't he tell me?" I try to swallow my alarm, conceal it from her, but I can feel my cheeks burning.

"Does he always have to check in with you, Darcy?" she asks softly.

"I would have prepared Kat," I said. "This is going to be hard for her."

"I'm sure your dad will do that."

"I'm sure he won't," I blurt out, giving away more than I intend to.

Ms. Wetzell studies me a moment too long. "I know you're not a guy who likes to talk about stuff, Darcy, but have you thought of keeping a journal, so you can record your feelings about the things in your life?"

"Haven't you heard?" I ask. "I don't have feelings."

It takes every bit of control I have not to slam the door on my way out.

THE HOURS AT Sammy's house seem twice as long as usual. I have to admit, it's Kat who mostly entertains Sam, and without her I have to work a lot harder.

Fortunately Star keeps her entertained for a while, but I'm getting a little tired of dressing stupid Barbie dolls by the time Mr. K gets home.

I thinks Mr. K's a little taken aback by how fast I'm out of there tonight. We often have a visit, in sign language, to brush up his skills, but I need to get home and find out if Kat is okay.

I find her sitting with Dad at the kitchen table. They each have a bowl of soup in front of them and I spot an empty can on the counter. The scene is so peaceful that a stranger would never guess this is not a typical family moment. Kat jumps up and greets Star as soon as we come in the door. I check her face for signs of tears. She looks perfectly okay.

"Well?" I ask her, signing and speaking at the same time, for Dad's benefit. "Are you okay?"

"Yeah, I'm fine," she signs, returning to the table.

"And?" I ask.

She smiles. "It's okay, Darcy," she signs. "I met her. She seems nice."

I stare at her, waiting for more, some rush of emotion, some hysterics. She goes back to eating her soup.

"She's changed a lot," Dad says. "She's like a different woman."

I plunk myself down at the table. "What do you mean?"

"She's been drug free for a long time. She's no longer paranoid or worried about where she's going to find her next fix. It's made her really calm compared to her former self."

"I thought you said she's borderline crazy."

He shrugs. "Maybe not."

I watch him slurp up a mouthful of tomato soup. "Why didn't you tell me you were taking Kat there today?"

"I didn't know until this morning. I had a light load, so I knew I'd be finished work early. Today seemed as good as any."

"What did you guys do?"

"Just sat around and visited."

Kat must have read his lips. She drops her spoon and begins to sign. "She's really good at signing," she says, way too enthusiastically for my liking. "She's been practicing, just for me."

Something snaps in my head. Here they are talking about my mother as if she's just come back from an extended holiday, all refreshed and ready to carry on. I can't stand it.

"That woman tried to kill you!" I tell Kat. "Her learning sign language doesn't make that fact go away!" I turn to Dad. "And if you think she's so wonderful and calm and safe and uncrazy now, why don't you invite her to come and live with you here? You think it's fine to dump Kat on her, but what about you? Are you willing to live with her again?"

I can't stand the tragic look on Kat's face. I push away from the table and nearly trip over Star. It's too much. With a swift kick the dog is out of my way and I'm back out the door.

DAD PULLS UP beside me when I'm walking home from
school. The Kippensteins are home this week with
Sammy. Kat's been going over to Mom's place every
day after school and Mom's parole officer supervises
their visits. Me? I'm out playing sports, hangin' with
my friends, having a regular holiday.

Right.

"Hop in."

I toss my pack into the backseat and climb in.

"She wants to see you," he says, pulling back out
into traffic.

"Not a chance."

"C'mon, Darcy. Do it for Kat."

"Forget it, Dad. I have nothing to say to her."

"Listen, Darcy, you might as well get this over with.
Kat is enjoying her visits, so I'd say if you don't make
some kind of peace with her, you're not going to get to
see much of Kat."

I don't have an answer for that. I've seen how con-
tent Kat is when she comes home from visiting her
each afternoon. Things are working out for Dad, for
Mom and for Kat. Of course, I don't count. All the
years of being there for Kat? Forgotten already.

Dad's right, though. I am going to have to go
eventually, even if it's just to pick Kat up or drop her
off sometime.

"All right." I try to sound resigned, but my heart
starts slamming around in my chest. What will she be
like? Will I remember her at all?

Will I feel like killing her?

A few minutes later Dad pulls up in front of an apartment tower. "Suite #504," he says.

"You're not coming?"

"No, Darcy. This is something I think you need to face on your own. Besides, Kat's already there, and so is the parole officer."

I look up, counting the floors until I reach the fifth one. Nothing but empty balconies. I'm surprised she'd take another fifth floor apartment.

"I'll be back for you in a couple of hours."

I find the apartment numbers and a phone on a wall plate beside the front door. Each number has a corresponding name beside it, except for Mom's. The place for her name has been left blank. I pick up the phone and press in the number. I'd rather be just about anywhere else at this moment, even in the dentist's chair, having all my teeth removed. Without anesthetic.

"Hello?"

"It's me, Darcy."

There's a pause. "Hi, Darcy."

A long beep. The door unlocks. I enter the building and push the button for the elevator.

She better not get too close to me.

The elevator doors slide open and I step inside and press the button. The doors shut again and I watch the floor indicator as the compartment climbs past them. Two. Three. Four. I don't want to be here. Five.

The door slides open, I step off and then Kat is there, wrapping her arms about me in a huge hug. A flood of emotion overcomes me. I shut my eyes, willing the tears to go back to where they came from.

I feel Kat's warm hand in mine, tugging me. "C'mon, Darcy," she encourages, pulling me down the corridor.

I allow myself to be led.

Then I see her, standing in an open doorway at the end of the hall. Ten years melt away in an instant. She's standing there, cigarette in hand, telling me I can come back now. I'm pushing baby Kat up and down the hallway in her stroller. Mom has a friend over and needs me to keep Kat happy while he's there. I'm delighted to have the responsibility, jiggling the buggy if she starts to whimper. I'll get candy later, if I do a good job. When I see her friend leave I can bring Kat back in. It doesn't take long. It never does. I hope I get Smarties. Or maybe a jawbreaker.

"Hi, Darcy," she says when we reach the end of the hallway.

I'm dropped back into the present with a thud. She's still standing in the doorway, arms crossed, smoke from her cigarette curling up past her face. She's smaller than I remember. I glance quickly at her face, but look away. Her eyes are Kat's eyes, only a million years older and sadder. I just nod. I have no voice.

"C'mon in," she says, stepping aside. Her voice sounds a little shaky. She better not start crying. I'm out of here if she does.

I enter the small apartment, stepping past the tiny kitchen and into the living room. The furniture is old, but the room looks comfortable. A woman who must be the parole officer is sitting in the far corner with a book. She looks up and nods. I nod back and she resumes reading, trying to look invisible. There's a plate of cookies on the coffee table and recent school photos of both Kat and me on top of the TV.

"Katrina brought them to me," Mom signs, indicating the pictures. Her signing is slow, but it's clear.

I just nod again and sink onto the couch. Kat sits beside me, looking anxious. I guess she's worried that I'll do something stupid and shake up this tenuous relationship she has established with her mom; the mom who once tried to kill her. Maybe I should.

"Would you like a Coke?" Mom asks with her hands. "And help yourself to a cookie. Kat and I baked them while we were waiting for you."

I glance at Kat and she nods proudly. How nice. Mom and daughter baking together. A Kodak moment, I'm sure.

"No, thanks," I say. I'm not participating in any of this.

She sits down on a chair facing us. She stubs out her cigarette in an ashtray. Her hair is pulled back into a ponytail and she's barefoot, wearing only jeans and a pale yellow T-shirt. She looks exactly the way I remember her. An ugly conflict begins to stir inside me. It's like I've been transported back in time, and the feelings I had for her as a little boy are trying to sneak out of the place they've been stashed for ten years. The grown-up me roughly pushes them away. Those little boy feelings didn't know better.

"Kat's been telling me that you're a wonderful big brother."

I glance at Kat. "Someone had to take care of her."

She nods sadly. "That's for sure."

It isn't the reaction I was hoping for.

"I know you're mad at me, Darcy. You have every right to be."

I don't say anything. What is there to say?

"I was hoping you'd give me a fresh start," she continues, using her hands and speaking slowly.

"Why should I?"

She shakes her head. "Because I need you to."

The phone rings.

"Hello?"

I watch Mom's face pale. She hangs up.

"Another one?" Kat asks.

Mom nods.

The phone rings again. I see the parole officer look up. Mom reaches for it but Kat jumps up. "No!" she says. She picks up the receiver and pushes it under a cushion on the couch.

Mom laughs. "You're catching on, Babe," she signs.

Babe? I'm about to barf.

"Mean people keep phoning and bugging Mom," Kat tells me.

She should tell someone who cares.

"Do you remember much about our life, Darcy? Before…before I went to prison?"

"Enough." That's an understatement, considering the memory that rushed back at me when I got off the elevator.

"I was a mess, wasn't I? I can't believe it was me when I look back on those days. It's like looking into someone else's nightmare." She lights another cigarette.

Kat tries to lighten the mood. "Mom says I can have a sleepover here next weekend," she tells me.

I look at her. "Oh yeah?" God, a whole weekend without her? I'm not ready for it. "What are you going to do with your dog?"

"You'll look after the dog, won't you, Darcy?" Mom asks.

"But she's mine," Kat argues. I see the signs of a puberty moment coming on. I can't believe she hasn't thought of this before now. "Dad just got her for me. Her name is Star, and I've just started training her to sense when I'm about to have a seizure and to protect me. Especially when Darcy's not there."

I glance at Mom's pale face. "You remember about the epilepsy, don't you?" I ask, pointedly.

I don't think she catches my meaning. She crosses one leg over the other and her foot begins to twitch nervously.

Kat glances about her. "I can bring her here, can't I?" she asks, her own alarm beginning to register on her face.

"Kat," Mom says, resting her cigarette on the ashtray so she can sign, "I don't think I'm allowed to have dogs here. It's such a small place."

Kat slumps a little lower on the couch. I hear the parole officer turn a page in her book.

"It's a big responsibility to have Kat for a whole weekend," I tell Mom. "She has to take medication for her seizures, but occasionally she gets them anyway. Are you sure you're up to it?"

But Mom's still thinking about the dog. "Kat, I'm going to be straightforward. I've promised myself to always be honest with you." She picks up the cigarette and takes a long pull on it. Her hand is shaking. "I'm afraid of dogs. Deathly afraid. Have been since I was a little girl and got this." She pulls up one leg of her jeans to expose a mass of scars twisting around her leg. It looks a lot like the underside of my arm. For a brief second I wonder if it really was a dog, but then I notice the shaking hand again.

"You were attacked?"

Mom nods.

"But Star isn't like that!" Kat signs. "She's gentle and sweet and—"

"It's an irrational fear, honey. The same way other people are afraid of spiders or snakes. I've tried to deal with it, but I've had to face up to so many other things. That one hasn't been high on my list."

"You'll get used to her," Kat insists. "I promise."

Mom stares at her. "I don't know. One thing at a time I think. We're just starting to get to know each other and I want to get reacquainted with your brother and find a job. There's so much for me to do already."

Kat sighs. I can see from her expression that Mom's hero-status has just taken a giant nosedive in Kat's estimation. It's like in the game of Snakes and Ladders when you almost get to the top to win, but then you land on that last snake and it swoops you down, practically back to square one. I'd say Mom's just made that slide.

Mom knows it too. I try hard not to look smug.

Seven

Kat decides not to visit Mom the next day, so we're home after school with Dad and with too much time on our hands. Kat mopes about the house, Star constantly at her side.

Dad finally gets fed up. "What is the matter with her?" he shouts at me after Kat has burst into tears for the fourth time.

"I think she's trying to decide which she wants more, a mom or a dog."

"Tell her she doesn't have a choice."

"You tell her. The dog was your idea."

"I'd forgotten about Sherri's stupid fears," he admits, then adds, mumbling, "God, you'd think she'd have outgrown it by now."

"I told you that you'd regret this, Dad."

He doesn't say a word.

I'M SURPRISED WHEN Kat decides to do the weekend sleepover. She's pulled herself together, and on Thursday night she packs a bag to take on Friday. She'll go straight to Mom's after school.

"You promise to feed and walk Star?" she signs, for the umpteenth time. Her anxious face makes my heart ache.

I nod and wonder how this is all going to resolve itself. I'm actually surprised that Dad hasn't called and asked Eileen to come and collect the damn dog.

Kat must have read my thoughts. "And I'll never forgive you if Dad gives her back while I'm away," she says.

"Dad blew it, Kat," I tell her, using my hands. "He should have checked with Mom before he got the dog. We both knew that."

"I'm going to make Mom change her mind," she signs back. "If she can stop using drugs she can stop being afraid of dogs."

I hand her the epilepsy medicine. "Some things you just can't change, Kat, no matter how badly you want to."

"That's what you think," she signs and drops the bottle into her new purse.

THE DEEP ACHE in my chest worsens when it's time to say goodbye to Kat on Friday morning. It is a pain that just will not go away. Maybe that's why I actually strike up a conversation with Gem. I can't find any other explanation.

I find her reading a book in the library at lunchtime and sit down beside her. She glances at me, surprised, but she doesn't tell me where to go, like I figured she would. God knows I deserve it.

"So how come you got sent to this school?" I ask, like we're old friends.

She closes her book and frowns. "What's got into you?"

"It's just a simple question."

"Nothing's simple when it comes to you, Darcy," she answers. "I'd say you're about as complicated as they come."

"Really. So now you're a psychoanalyst or something?"

"Doesn't take a psychoanalyst to know you're one antisocial guy."

I decide not to argue with that.

"So, what do you want?" she asks.

It's a good question. I don't know, really. I just felt the need to talk to someone, to build one of those damn bridges or something. It's not a feeling I'm used to. When I open my mouth to speak, I'm amazed at what comes out. "I'm dog-sitting for my sister this weekend. I thought maybe you could help me. You seemed to like her better than I do."

"You don't like that dog?" She looks incredulous.

"It's not that I don't like her. I just…I don't know. I've never given dogs or what to do with them much thought. Besides, I didn't like all the attention she got when I was out walking her. You're probably friendlier than me."

"Probably?" she laughs. "I sure hope so!"

I can't help myself. I smile.

"Whoa," she says. "Do you ever look different when you smile."

She's studying me in a way that makes me feel squirmy. I have to look away.

"Sure," she says. "Why don't we take her to that field down by the creek and see if she likes to play fetch? I'll bring a tennis racket and some old balls."

"Okay," I agree. "As long as you promise not to go reciting any of The Rose's quotes on me."

She smacks my arm.

"This afternoon?" I ask.

"This afternoon."

I notice the ache in my heart begins to ease, just a little.

I SPOT HER coming across the field toward us. The wind is whipping her hair around her head. She's wearing a denim jacket with fleece lining. The collar is up to keep her neck warm. Her stride is confident and she waves a gloved hand when she spots me. Star sees her too and sniffs the air. I think she recognizes her. Her tail starts wagging hard.

Gem shows Star a tennis ball. "You know how to play fetch, girl? Do you?" I notice she talks to Star in a high-pitched voice, as if she's talking to a two-year- old kid, and I swear Star knows exactly what Gem's suggesting because her tail gets wagging so hard that it pulls her in circles. She barks at Gem and then bends forward, her rear end in the air, her long feathered tail as steady as a metronome.

Gem whacks the ball across the field and Star charges after it. We watch her quietly. In less than a minute she's back, dropping the ball neatly at Gem's feet. "Good girl!" Gem says. She picks up the ball and slams it with the racket again. Star's gone like a shot. They keep this up for a good fifteen minutes, and despite some serious panting, Star shows no sign of quitting. Finally she comes back, drops the ball a short distance from Gem and flops down beside it, chest heaving. She doesn't lift her head, but her eyes roll to look up at Gem apologetically.

Gem laughs. "It's okay, Star. I know you need a rest."

I've been watching the game quietly, but now I feel awkward. Without Star to watch I'm going to have to think of something intelligent to say. "Thanks," I say, for starters. "That did the trick. And I didn't have to be friendly, either."

"You're not off the hook yet, buddy. You'll be out walking her again before the evening's over."

"That's not what I wanted to hear."

I'm still watching Star, but I sense Gem studying my face again. I wonder what she's thinking. "Do you want to walk along the creek?" I ask, surprising even myself.

"Sure."

Star climbs to her feet and follows us as we tromp down to the path that follows the water's edge. I don't bother with the leash but let her wander along beside us, sniffing at who knows what.

"You never answered my question this afternoon," I say.

"What question was that?"

"Why you're at Hope Springs Alternate. "

I feel her mood shift and immediately regret asking the question. "You don't have to tell me," I mumble.

"It's okay," she says. We continue walking. "I guess I'm just like most of the kids there," she says quietly. "I couldn't handle the rules at my last school. I was always late, I could never get my assignments done on time and I was just kinda flunking out. It's weird. I didn't try to get in trouble, but I couldn't organize myself the way they expected us to."

I nod, urging her to continue.

"Then I started hanging out with other kids who didn't fit the norm." She pauses, thinking about it. "Things got out of hand. We did some really stupid stuff." She kicks the toe of her shoe into the gravel path. "I wish I could go back and erase most of it."

I have no idea how to respond, so I don't say anything.

"How 'bout you?" she asks. "You seem pretty organized."

"I'm not quite sure why I'm there," I tell her. "I think it had more to do with my personality than anything else."

"Yeah, well, you are a bit different," she says. "But I've always liked different."

I glance at her. Is she saying she likes me? The sparkle is back in her eyes and I feel myself relax a little.

"So," she says, changing the subject, "is your sister going to keep Star?"

"I don't know. Dad wants Kat to go live with our mom, but Mom is afraid of dogs. Kat's totally in love with the dog, but she wants things to work out with Mom, too."

"She's got a bit of a problem."

"Just a bit."

"Are you going to live with your mom too?"

"Not a chance."

"Why not?"

"Like you don't know?" I don't like the direction this conversation is moving in.

"Your sister doesn't have a problem with it."

"Well, I do." I try to think of a way to change the subject, but I'm at a loss for words.

"What's she like, anyway?"

"My mom?"

"Yeah."

"She's a bitch. What do you think? She dropped her baby daughter off a balcony."

"Then why does your sister want to live with her?"

"I guess she's tired of living with just me and my dad. She wants a mom."

Gem arranges the tin of balls and racket in one arm and picks up a stick with the other. She flings it toward the river. Star must have thought the games had started again because she goes charging through the brush to retrieve it. The stick hits the water with a splash. So does Star. She's dropping the stick at Gem's feet a moment later. Gem chucks it again.

"What do you remember?"

I feel a sweat break out in my pits, even though the wind is cold. "I remember baby-sitting Kat in the hall of our apartment building while she entertained men inside. I was all of four years old. Nice, huh?"

She gives me a sad look, which only pisses me off. "And then after she tries to kill my sister she goes to jail and leaves us with a man who doesn't want us."

"Did you love her back then?" she asks quietly.

"Well, duh. I was just a little kid. She was my mom. I didn't know any better."

"Maybe you can learn to love her again."

Star drops the stick at Gem's feet, but I pick it up before she does and wing it as hard as I can. Star bounds away after it. "She doesn't deserve my love." I shove my hands deep into my pockets, trying to control the rage I feel building up inside of me.

"You know, things are not always what they seem. It sounds like your mom would like to erase some of the stuff she did too," Gem says.

"It's a little late now."

She looks directly at me. "Yeah," she says. "I guess it is."

Star returns without the stick. Her body breaks into a tremendous shudder, starting with her head and shoulders, and ending with the tip of her tail. Gem and I jump back, but not quickly enough. We are covered in water. I guess Star has had enough of this little party. So have I. I turn around and lead the way back.

It's Saturday night. Dad's out. Star is sitting across the living room from me, staring out the window. She's probably watching for Kat to come home.

"Star," I say quietly. She turns, looking at me with sad eyes. "She's not coming."

She cocks her head.

"You've been left behind."

Her ears perk forward and she tilts her head the other way.

"Trust me on this one, Star. That's what they do."

With a little whimper, she pads across the floor and places her head on my knee. I console her by massaging her ears, just the way I saw Gem do it.

Mom phones Dad on Sunday afternoon and tells him that Kat is anxious for me to come with him to pick her up. Apparently she has something to show me. Reluctantly, I climb into the car. When we arrive at the apartment building I look up and see Kat watching for us from the balcony. I step out of the car and wave to her. She leans against the rail, pressing something to her chest. It moves.

"Look, Darcy!" she yells. "Mom got me a kitten."

I swear my heart stops beating. I gawk up at her and see the kitten squirming in her arms. Kat's too close to the edge but too excited about the kitten to wait for me to get upstairs to see it up close. Panic grips me. I want to run up those five flights and yank her off the balcony, but my boots are cemented to the pavement. I try to yell at her, tell her to get away from the rail, but nothing but a dry cough comes out of my mouth.

"Darcy?" Kat yells down. "Are you okay?"

A blur of cloudy images blinds me. A baby is falling, falling. A woman's tortured wails sear the still air and a small boy watches quietly from the balcony. I scrunch up my eyes and cover my ears. I don't want to see any more. I don't want to hear any more. MAKE IT GO AWAY! a voice in my head screams.

"What is it, Darcy?" Dad's voice cuts through the screaming in my head. "Are you okay?"

With a great effort I force my eyes open and uncover my ears, but I have no voice. I can't see anything. I can only shake my head. No, I'm not okay.

"You're pale," he says. "Let's get upstairs before you pass out on the sidewalk."

He pushes me toward the door and my feet miraculously unglue themselves from the ground. I feel like I can't get enough air. I suck in huge gulps. Dizziness and nausea overwhelm me. Everything is black except for little white sparks that are flashing in my head.

Dad puts his hand on my back and pushes me to the elevator. I swallow hard, trying not to throw up.

In Mom's apartment I flop onto the couch. She brings me a glass of water. I close my eyes and lie back. A moment later I feel a cool cloth gently wiping my forehead. It is accompanied by that fragrance, the one Ms. LaRose wears...

I push Mom away and sit up.

"What is it, Darcy?" Kat asks. I can see her now. She is still holding the little gray kitten in her arms. The kitten is staring at me, wide eyed. I glance around. Mom and Dad are staring at me too.

I clear my throat, hoping my voice has returned. "I don't know," I lie. "I just felt sick all of a sudden."

"You were fine until you stepped out of the car," Dad says, "and saw Kat on the balcony..."

An awkward hush comes over the room. The kitten mews and Kat places it on the floor. I glance at Mom. Something passes between us. She knows what I saw. What I remembered. But is that really the way it happened? I swallow hard and look away.

The kitten jumps onto the side of the couch, its tiny nails making ripping sounds in the fabric.

"Isn't she cute?" Kat signs at me.

"Is the kitten supposed to replace Star?" I ask her.

"No!" Kat signs, frowning.

"I'm not trying to replace the dog," Mom says. "I just wanted Kat, and you too, to have a pet here."

"Don't worry about me." I'm still feeling shaky, but I'm also pissed off. "I won't be hanging out here."

Now Dad clears his throat. "Are you all right then?" he asks.

I take a deep, shuddering breath and nod.

"Then tell Kat to say goodbye." He picks up the bag she's left in the narrow hallway and steps out the door.

I glance once more at Mom, wondering what the truth is. The images that hit me on the sidewalk are already fading, and now I'm not sure if I can believe

what I saw. She's still studying me, looking concerned.
I tell Kat we're leaving and follow Dad out the door.

WE'RE BACK AT Samantha's on Tuesday afternoon, Kat,
myself and Star. Nothing has been resolved; no one
is even talking about what comes next in the ongoing
saga of Mom and Kat. I, in turn, refuse to acknowledge
the images that hit me on the sidewalk under Mom's
balcony. I must have been imagining things.

"How was your holiday?" I ask Mrs. K as she gets
ready to leave.

She doesn't answer right away. She watches Sammy
and Kat playing with Star and then turns to me,
thoughtfully. "It was a good rest, I guess, but I still
don't know what's going on with Sammy. I guess she
just doesn't have the vocabulary or sign language to
tell us. But she was really looking forward to seeing
you two again. You three," she adds, glancing at Star.

I nod, reassured that my job is a little more secure
than it was a week ago. "Kat's been acting kind of
weird too," I tell her. "Maybe it's the way the planets
are lined up or something."

Mrs. K smiles, but the frown is back by the time she
heads out the door.

BY THURSDAY MRS. K is getting really concerned about
Sammy. She takes me aside and asks if I've noticed
anything unusual about Sam's behavior. I have to admit, she is getting harder to handle. For one thing,
she refuses to take a bath for me, something she's

always enjoyed. Now she has a total hissy fit as soon as I sign the word.

Mrs. K fills me in on some of the other stuff Sammy's been doing. "She keeps drawing stick-man-type pictures of people, and…" Mrs. K looks uncomfortable, "the male private parts are always, you know… there. And emphasized. Exaggerated."

"Oh." What else can I say?

"Her preschool teachers just laugh and say that all four-year-old girls go through a period of penis envy," Mrs. K continues. She glances at me. "That's a Freudian theory. Freud was a psychologist in the nineteenth century. Have you studied him in school yet?"

I shake my head.

"But I don't know," she continues, without going into more detail on the theories of dead people. "Yesterday I took her to McDonald's and there was a mannequin of Ronald McDonald standing there." Mrs. K closes her eyes briefly and takes a deep breath. "She asked me if he had one."

I don't have to ask what she means by "one." I do, though, have to fight the urge to laugh. It was, I thought, a good question, and it reminded me of an old joke I'd heard.

"Do you know how to identify Ronald McDonald on a nudist beach?" I ask, trying to change the topic. She just shakes her head, looking confused.

"He's the one with sesame seeds on his buns."

Her face is blank and I immediately regret telling it. I'd forgotten how stupid the punch line was.

"And today," Mrs. K continues as if I hadn't said a thing, "she was watching reruns of Mr. Rogers on TV and she asked if he…well, you know."

That, I thought, wasn't so funny. I spent my first five years planted in front of the TV. Each day Mr. Rogers brought a comforting, calm half hour to my life, which was filled with images of anguish and despair from the daytime TV I watched with Mom. "You are special," he always said, and how I wanted to believe him. Even Mom hung onto his gentle, consoling words. When no one else cared, we always knew he did.

Of course he had one.

"I really don't know what to do about all this," Mrs. K says. "If I could talk to her more easily…" she sighs. "I have an appointment for her tomorrow. I'll see what the doctor says."

"I bet the preschool teachers are right," I say for lack of anything intelligent to suggest, and still feeling embarrassed about my poor taste in jokes. "It's probably just one of those phases kids go through."

Finally Mrs. K smiles, just a little. "You're pretty wise for a young man who hasn't raised any kids yet." I laugh politely, but don't tell her how wrong she is. I've been raising Kat for eleven years.

GEM HAS BEEN joining me in the library at break and lunch. We don't talk much, just sit side by side listening to CDs. Sometimes she'll recommend one she likes, but that's about the extent of our conversation. Today, though, she breaks the comfortable silence.

"Are you dog-sitting again this weekend?" she asks as we walk back to class.

"Yeah, I'm afraid I am." Was she going to offer to help me again? I try to ignore the tingle of excitement that races through me at the thought.

"Do you want me to come by and get her, you know, take her off your hands for a while? Give you a little break?

"Oh. Yeah, sure." Act cool. Act cool.

"Or we could go back to the creek if you want," she says, looking closely at my face.

Has she seen my disappointment? Shit!

"Whatever," I say.

"No. You decide."

"Okay, then you come and get her."

She nods. "I will." She sounds disappointed.

What is the matter with me?

Eight

The phone wakes me up Saturday morning. Dad must be home because it only rings twice. As soon as I stir, the dog's standing at the side of my bed, looking anxious. When Kat's at Mom's place, Star sleeps in my room. I didn't invite her to; she's just there when I go to bed. It makes no difference to me.

"I know, I know. You need to pee." Unwillingly I get up, wondering at what point I succumbed to actually talking out loud to this dog. "You're just going to have to wait your turn," I continue, defeated. "I'm first."

Dad's hanging up the phone when I go into the kitchen. "Who called?" I ask. I wonder if it was Gem. She was planning to take Star for a walk this morning.

He responds by whacking me in the side of the head. I have to grab the kitchen counter to keep my balance.

"Hey!"

"Just when I think I'm going to get my life back you have to go screw everything up!" he yells.

"What did I do?" I rub my head, confused. Star is standing at the door, whimpering.

"Like you don't know?" His face is right up to mine. His breath reeks.

"No, I don't."

"How about that cute little deaf brat you baby-sit? Does that jog your memory?"

"What has Sammy got to do with anything?"

"Don't act stupid with me."

"I'm not! What's going on?"

He just glares at me. Star barks. "Take that fuckin' dog out, but don't be gone long," he orders. "We're expecting company."

I don't move. "Not till you tell me what's going on."

"I've been told not to say a thing. I've said too much already," he growls. "Now do as you're told."

Grabbing Star's leash I head out the door and down the stairs. My head is reeling. What's got into him? He's not the world's best parent, but to his credit, he's never hit either of us. Until now.

I walk slowly, being in no rush to face Dad's mysterious rage again, and hoping my own anger will begin to simmer down. As I come back along our street I see an unmarked police car pull up in front of our townhouse. The Kippensteins and a female cop climb out of it. I also see Gem coming down the street from the other direction. We all arrive at the bottom of the stairs at the same time.

"Hey, what's up?" I ask the Kippensteins.

They completely ignore me. Their faces are like masks, angry masks, and Mr. K steers his wife up the stairs. Dad opens the door as if he was expecting them and they go in. I glance at the cop and find her studying me. She doesn't look like a happy camper either.

"What's going on?" Gem asks quietly.

"I haven't a clue."

"Do you still want me to walk the dog?"

"Yeah, please." I hand her the leash and feel a small jolt run up my arm as her hand accidentally brushes mine. I must be losing it. "And phone before you bring her back. Hopefully this little party will be over by then."

She searches my face. "Are you okay?"

I nod.

"Get up here now, Darcy!" Dad bellows from the top of the stairs.

"Good luck," she whispers, after glancing at Dad. I watch her walk down the sidewalk with Star, who glances back at me, her tail hanging forlornly between her legs.

The cop has gone up the stairs ahead of me.

"Is someone going to tell me what's going on?" I ask, joining them in the kitchen, but before anyone can answer, a horrible thought blindsides me. "Has something happened to Sammy?"

Everyone's angry eyes are on me but no one says a thing.

"What is it?" I demand.

"Samantha's been sexually assaulted," the cop says, regarding me carefully.

My heart bangs against my rib cage. The vision of someone doing something like that to Sammy is too repugnant for words. Then the truth hits me. "You think it was me?" I feel like I'm going to throw up.

"Sammy told us it was you," Mrs. K says. I hear the tremble in her voice. She's gritting her teeth.

"I don't believe it! What exactly did she say?"

Mrs. Kippenstein lets out a ragged sigh. "She couldn't really tell me, of course. She doesn't have enough words or know enough sign language. So I took some paper and she helped me draw what happened. Between that and a little charades I got the whole story."

"And she said it was me?" I repeat.

Mrs. K looks down at her hands. "I asked if it was you and she said it was."

"Why would she say that?" I demand. "She's like my own sister. I would never do anything to her!"

"Where is your little sister?" the cop asks. "We need to talk to her, too."

"Katrina's at her mother's for the weekend," Dad tells her.

She looks surprised but she doesn't say anything.

"I need to talk to Sam," I tell the group. "To find out why she's saying this."

Mr. K lurches to his feet, practically knocking his chair over in the process. He leans toward me, his hands clenched at his sides, his face blotchy red. "You go anywhere near Samantha and I'll…"

He leaves that threat unfinished, but his anger is contagious. I stand and face him. "I resent being accused of something I didn't do." I feel my own fists clenching. "If I can talk to her I'll find out what's really going on."

"Sit down, Darcy," the cop says, firmly pushing us away from each other. "We need to investigate this further."

Without losing eye contact with me, Mr. K drops back into his chair, but my adrenaline is pumping so hard there's no way I can sit still. I pace the kitchen, trying to control my breathing, willing my racing heart to slow down.

"Now," she continues, ignoring my agitation, "I need to get an interpreter so I can talk to Samantha myself."

"I can interpret," Mrs. K says. She pulls a tissue out of her purse and she wipes her nose.

"No, we need someone completely unbiased," the woman says. "And then I'd like the interpreter to talk to Darcy's sister, Katrina."

I'm wondering how this cop already knows so much about us. "What's Kat got to do with anything?"

She speaks calmly. "The Kippensteins tell me you have a very close relationship with your sister."

"Yeah, and?"

"She baby-sits with you."

"Oh. So now you think she's in on this too? Don't make me sick."

"It's all part of a thorough investigation."

"Leave Kat out of this. She doesn't need to hear this kind of shit."

"Darcy!" My dad, the man with the filthy mouth, acts offended at my language.

"She doesn't! It's a bunch of crap."

The room is quiet. My dad is glaring at me. The Kippensteins are watching the cop, who is making notes in a small book.

"Darcy, you're to stay completely away from Samantha Kippenstein until this investigation is complete," she says.

"You don't need to worry about that." I refuse to look at the Kippensteins. I can't believe they'd accuse me of doing anything to hurt Sam.

"Will Katrina's mother be willing to keep Katrina with her until I've finished my investigation?" she asks Dad.

He nods. "Probably."

"How long can this possibly take?" I ask. "You'll get an interpreter to talk to the girls today and then you'll find out there's been some big mistake."

"Hopefully that'll be the case," she says. "I'm just covering all my bases." She pushes back her chair and stands to leave. "I'll be in touch."

The Kippensteins' follow her out the door, shutting it firmly behind them. I'm left with Dad and a horrible silence.

"I didn't do anything," I tell him, finally.

"Yeah? Then why did the kid say you did?"

"I don't know. But I didn't."

"We'll see about that, won't we. In the meantime, you're grounded. No phone calls, no friends over, no nothing. You're not to leave this house except to go to school."

I just stare at him. How can he be so stupid? Has he never noticed that I don't get phone calls or visitors anyway? I slide by his bulk in the doorway and slam shut the door to my room. I hear the front door slam in response, and then the engine of his car revs into life. I open my drawer and pull out my knife. Stepping out of my body, I watch myself cut.

I STAY IN my room the rest of the weekend, mostly sleeping or staring at the ceiling. The phone keeps ringing— it's probably Gem wanting to return the dog—but I don't answer it. I study the fresh wounds on my arms and realize that the cutting hasn't solved much. How could anyone hurt Sammy? And why would Sammy say I did it? There's no doubt that she's been abused—it explains all her strange behavior—but why say it was me? Is she scared to tell the truth for some reason? And do the Kippensteins really think I'd do something like that? I can't believe it. They trusted me with their daughter. I thrived on their trust.

The answer hits me hard. It's because of my mom. They think I've turned out bad because she's bad. I pull the blankets over my head.

LATE SUNDAY AFTERNOON I hear the doorbell ring and then my dad calls me into the living room. The cop is standing there, looking grim.

"What?"

"An interpreter has spoken with both your sister and Samantha Kippenstein."

"Yeah, and?"

"I think you'd better sit down, Darcy."

I glance at my dad. He won't make eye contact with me. He pulls a cigarette from his pack and lights it. I slump onto the couch. I feel a sick sensation deep in my gut. The cop sits down in Dad's armchair and faces me.

"What does Samantha call you, Darcy?"

I think about that. Kat and I understand her speech, and so do her parents, but I doubt anyone else would. "She tries to say Darcy," I tell the woman, "my Darcy, but it comes out garbled."

"And when she's signing? What word does she use then?"

Usually we're signing directly to each other so we don't need to use names, but I remember Kat using the sign for the letter D to talk about me to Sam. I tell the cop that, wondering about the point of her question.

She nods and then glances at my dad. "Samantha is still saying that the person who…who hurt her is the person she calls D."

My dad erupts. "You stupid little ass! I can't believe my own flesh and blood…"

"That's enough, Mr. Fraser," the officer says with a sharp glance at him.

I feel the blood rushing from my head, leaving me dizzy.

"The interpreter has also spoken with your sister," the policewoman continues.

"Don't tell me," my father says.

"Your sister says you've had sexual relations with her, too."

Dad lurches toward me, his face purple with rage, but the cop jumps to her feet and blocks Dad's path. She doesn't say a thing. She doesn't have to. Dad glares at me, but retreats to his corner. I guess he figures he can wait until she's gone.

I'm too stunned to say a thing. It's like knowing you're having a horrific nightmare, but not being able to wake yourself up from it.

"She told you that?" I finally blurt out.

"Through her interpreter, yes."

"Then she doesn't know what sexual relations are! I've never touched her! She's my sister!"

"Are you denying the accusations, Darcy?"

"Of course I am! I've never had sex with anyone, and I'm not about to start with my sister or a four-year-old girl. I don't know what the hell is going on!"

The cop looks back down at her notes. "Sometimes, Darcy, when brothers and sisters are real close, and then they reach puberty, their relationship becomes physical."

"You're making me sick."

"I'm just trying to understand what's going on."

"You're not doing a very good job."

"Okay. Then fill me in."

"I don't have a clue."

She studies me and then shrugs. "Given this information, I'm sure the Kippensteins will want to press charges."

"And how do I prove I'm innocent?"

"You'll be appointed a lawyer and a social worker."

"This isn't fair!" I yell at the cop. "I didn't do anything wrong!"

"You'll have an opportunity to prove that in court."

"NO!"

I can't sit here another minute. Back in my room I reach for my knife, but my arm is still too raw from my last cutting session, and besides, there's a good chance my dad will barge in, so instead I let my rage explode. I kick the door, the walls, the bed. I yank open my drawers and fling my clothes around, screaming every curse word I've ever heard, which is quite a repertoire. I stomp on the floor, making as much noise as possible. Eventually, when I find nothing else to toss, I lie face down on my bed, tormented and with no sense of release. The knife would have worked way better. I hear the front door closing and then the sound of the police cruiser pulling away from the curb. I expect Dad to bang through my bedroom door any minute.

I wait. And wait. Nothing.

Then I hear the front door slam shut again and another car pulls away. I guess Dad's decided to confront his anger with a pint of beer. Or three. Maybe he doesn't want to risk being labeled a child abuser. Mind you, it beats being labeled a sex offender.

I feel hot tears burning my eyes but I push them away. I lie on my bed and watch the light on the wall change as afternoon turns to evening, and evening turns to night. I force my mind to go blank and to think only about the light.

I FEEL NOTHING on Monday morning. Complete numbness. Dad's gone to work and I'm unsure of my status. If I'm to be charged with sexual abuse, can I still walk out the door and go to school? I don't bother, but go back to bed after eating a piece of toast.

The phone rings and rings. I can hear the answering machine kicking in but can't make out the voices. I drift in and out of sleep. Eventually there's a knock on the front door. I don't bother to answer it either, but the knocker perseveres. The knocking becomes a banging and I hear Mom calling my name.

I drag myself off the bed and go to the door.

"What do you want?"

"I just came to check up on you. The school is trying to track you down. They got hold of your dad and he phoned me and asked if I'd come and see you."

"Well, as you can see, I'm fine. You can leave now."

"You don't look fine."

"Thanks."

"I heard about the trouble you're in."

"I didn't do it." I turn and walk up the stairs. I can hear her following me.

"I know." She's followed me into the kitchen. I open the fridge door and pour myself a glass of milk. She sits at the table, looking around the room. It doesn't look like she's planning to leave anytime soon.

"So how do you know?" I ask, but not really caring. No one would believe her anyway.

"I just do."

"Great. That's really going to help me."

She doesn't answer.

"This is all your fault."

"Why's that?" She sits up a little straighter. I think maybe I've ticked her off. Good.

"Everyone's going to think I've turned out bad because you're bad."

"I'm not bad, Darcy. I was self-destructive before I went to prison, but I'm not bad."

"You tried to kill my sister. That's not bad?"

"I didn't try to kill your sister. It was an accident." She's looking at her hands.

The images that hit me on the sidewalk outside her apartment that day blindside me again. My stomach lurches. We're not going to discuss that day. Not now. Not ever. Things are bad enough already. "I'm going to bed."

"Darcy, we need to talk."

I'm already down the hall. "We have nothing to talk about." I slam the door to my room and flop facedown on the bed.

The door opens. I become aware of perfume again. Ms. LaRose's perfume. "Yes, we do," she says. I hear the chair from my desk slide out and then creak when she sits on it.

"First of all, Darcy, I want you to know that my years in prison were...were really good in a lot of ways."

"Huh?" I have to glance at her. She's talking crazy now.

"I had people taking care of me. I was being fed. I was being counseled. It felt like people were concerned about what was going to happen to me. That was a first."

"Yeah, well, while you were in prison being cared for, I was on the outside fending for myself and taking care of Kat." I bury my face in my pillow again.

The silence lasts so long that I begin to think she may have left. I lift my head and glance over at my desk. She's still there.

"The other day," she says, very quietly, "when you came to visit me, you remembered the...that day, didn't you." It's a statement, not a question.

"No!" I bury my face again. I won't go there. I won't I won't I won't.

"What do you remember, Darcy?"

"Nothing!"

"C'mon, Darcy. Talk to me."

"I can't remember anything," I tell her, trying to convince myself, but the images are coming back, vividly. "NO NO NO!" I shake my head, willing the memories to go away, but they're flooding my consciousness, forcing me back to that day. I remember a TV documentary…lab-coated guys dropping cats upside down from various heights while filmmakers captured the way they contorted—mid-fall—to land on their feet. The film clips were shown one frame at a time and I'd watched, fascinated, as the cats turned themselves and landed right side up…

I pull the blankets over my head, but it's too late.

I am that little boy again. Now Kat's little body is falling, falling…I remember every detail of her descent. It happened in slow motion, frame by frame…her arms are flailing, her body twisting…she's a fluttering leaf, ripped from a tree in a gust of wind…

A gasp startles me. I look back at Mom from the little patio table I'm perched on. Mom, standing in the doorway, covers her face with her hands. I peer back over the rungs of the railing just in time to see Kat's tiny body land—flat on her back—in the overgrown shrubs that crowd the sidewalk. For a moment she doesn't move, but then I see her tiny blonde head turn, and she looks up at us, wide eyed, shocked. Her mouth opens and I hear kitten-like mews…

Why is she on her back?

I slam back into the present, crouched on the bed, trembling. "SHE WAS SUPPOSED TO LAND ON HER FEET!" I scream at my mom. "HER NAME IS KAT!" Mom just stares at me, her face pale.

"Her name is Kat," I repeat, quieter now. "Cats land on their feet."

I cannot hold the sobs back. I'm choking on them. Years and years of grief pour out. I use my blanket to wipe my eyes, my nose. And then I feel the hand, rubbing soft circles on my back. The next thing I know she's holding me, and I'm sobbing into her neck. I can't stop. I can't. I just cry and cry and cry...

WE'RE SITTING AT the kitchen table. My hand shakes as I bring a can of pop to my mouth. I have never felt so completely empty, so spent. But something in my brain begins to tick again. There are questions I need the answers for. "So why did you let them send you to prison?"

She doesn't say anything.

"To protect me?"

I read her silence as a yes.

"I was just a little kid! They wouldn't have put me behind bars!"

Her voice is small, child-like. "I shook her."

"The epilepsy?"

She nods. "I think so." She sits quietly for another moment. "I take back what I said before. I guess I am bad after all."

We sit without saying anything.

"And you know, Darcy," she says finally, her voice shaking, "even if I didn't do it, I needed to do time. I was out of control. And as it turns out, it was the best thing that ever happened to me. I'm clean now."

I must look doubtful because she defends herself. "I am. And I've grown up. That wouldn't have happened if I hadn't been put away."

"But now everyone despises you. For something I did."

"Society despised me before." Her voice is flat, expressionless. "It makes no difference."

"I can't believe I forgot what really happened to Kat that day."

"You didn't."

No, I guess not. I take another gulp from my can. "Kat means everything to me."

"I know. And you've done an awesome job of being a big brother, so now you have to forgive yourself for what happened. Feeling guilty won't change anything."

We sit quietly again. I'm trying to reformat my brain. For so long I've hated my mom for trying to murder my sister. Now I find out—remember—that I did it. How am I supposed to feel about her now? How am I supposed to feel about me now?

"You said you believed me..." I can hardly say it. "About not hurting Kat and Sammy."

"That's right. I do."

"Why? They both said I did it."

"I know what it feels like to be wrongly accused of something."

"That still doesn't mean I didn't do it."

"That's true. But I think I'm a good judge of character, and I don't believe you'd do anything like that."

"I dropped my sister off a balcony."

"That's different. You weren't much more than a baby yourself."

Yeah. Right. As if that makes any difference.

Nine

Ms. LaRose comes banging on the door before Mom even leaves. They introduce themselves to each other, awkwardly. I'm shocked at the similarities between the two. I can't believe I didn't see it before. Their ages, their appearance, even the way they dress. Mom excuses herself, telling me she'll be back to see me in the morning.

"Does that mean you won't be at school again tomorrow?" The Rose asks once my mom is gone.

"I don't know what it means." I lean against the door, exhausted. I just want to go back to bed.

"I brought you some homework."

"Great. I was hoping you would." There I go again. I just can't help myself, but maybe she'll take the hint and leave.

Ms. LaRose looks at me intently. "You don't look well, Darcy."

"I don't feel well."

"What's happening?"

I look her in the eye. I can't even find the energy to lie. "I've had a crappy couple of days. Like real crappy."

She nods. "Sit down."

I do. I fold my arms on the table and rest my head on them. I close my eyes. I just want to sleep.

She sits across the table from me. "So, what's going on?" she asks gently.

"Well…" Where should I start? "I sexually assaulted a four-year-old girl," I tell her, not bothering to lift my head. "The deaf girl I baby-sit. And I also had sexual relations with my sister. Didn't you hear?"

"Cut the crap, Darcy," she says.

I look up, startled. She's never used that tone with me before. "Well that's what I've been accused of."

"Okay, so there's been some kind of terrible mistake. How did it happen?"

"If I knew that…"

She becomes quiet for a moment. "Right," she says finally. "Let's start with the little girl you baby-sit. What's her name?"

I sit up, but close my eyes for a moment. I don't want to deal with this now, not after what I've just been through with Mom.

I'm so tired.

I wish she'd leave.

"Samantha," I say, slumping down in my chair and crossing my arms. "But we call her Sammy or Sam for short."

"And she said you sexually assaulted her?"

She's not going to let up. I try to steel myself for the onslaught of questions that I sense is coming. "Apparently."

"Can you think of anything, any little thing," she says with emphasis, "that you may have done that could be misconstrued and considered sexual abuse?"

I can only shake my head. "I've been wondering about that for three whole days now."

"Does she dress herself?"

"I feel like there should be a light shining in my eyes, blinding me, the way they do it on TV interrogations."

"Just answer my questions, Darcy."

"What was the question?"

"Does she dress herself?"

"Mostly. Sometimes she needs help with buttons or figuring out which is the front and which is the back."

"How about baths? Are you responsible for them?"

"Yeah."

"And what do you do?"

"I run the water. She takes off her clothes and climbs in. We play with bath toys together, but that's about it."

"Do you wash her?"

"No. She washes herself, but I shampoo her hair sometimes."

"You never…touch her anywhere you shouldn't?"

"Fuck you!" I bury my face in my arms again, shocked at myself. I didn't mean to say that.

"Darcy," she says gently. "if you go to court the prosecutor is going to ask you these same questions, but not with the intention of helping you. I am trying to help you. I just want us to figure out how Samantha could have mistaken your actions for sexual abuse."

"I don't believe she did. We're buddies."

"But her parents are convinced you did something?"

"Uh-huh."

She sighs. "Okay, let's talk about your sister, then."

"Have you been hired as my lawyer or social worker or something?"

"No," she says quietly. "I'm just here as your friend. Someone who cares about you."

I hate it when people are nice to me. Now I feel the tears welling up in my eyes again. Where have they come from? I've always been able to push them away before, and besides, there should be none left after that scene with my mom. I cover my face with my hands. This is too embarrassing.

"Darcy," Ms. LaRose says sadly, "if it weren't considered so inappropriate, I'd be sitting beside you right now, hugging you. You know that, right?"

God, how I wish she was.

Neither of us says anything for a moment. By pressing my fingers into my eyes I manage to hold back the tears.

"Why do you believe me?" I ask eventually. How ironic that I asked my mom that same question about an hour ago.

"I don't know," she says finally. "I've worked with lots of kids over the years and you learn to see through the outward behavior after a while. I guess it's just the way I read you. You wouldn't do anything like that."

"Oh yeah. I'm such a sweet, loveable kind of guy."

"Sweet? No. Loveable? Yeah, I think so." I glance at her just long enough to see she's smiling at me. "I can read through that tough exterior of yours, Darcy. I know you've erected a solid rock wall to protect yourself, but you're not someone who would ever hurt little girls. That's very clear to me."

Rock walls? That quote was for my benefit. I suspected as much. "Then how come it isn't clear to everyone else? Like my dad, for example? He's lived with me all these years and he assumes I'm guilty."

"I don't know your dad, Darcy," she says, "but maybe he's not particularly sensitive."

"That's an understatement."

"So," she says, "back to your little sister. Did she say you had sex with her?"

My little sister. The little sister I tried to kill.

"Darcy?"

"Huh?"

"She said you had sex with her?"

"Apparently, but I don't believe she'd say that."

"It is strange, isn't it, that both girls have come forward and said these things at the same time?"

"They didn't actually 'come forward'," I tell her. "Sammy was acting weird. She was fixated on...on male body parts." I can't look Ms. LaRose in the eyes and say that. "So her mom questioned her about what was going on. Apparently that's when she said I did something."

I glance at Ms. LaRose. She just sits quietly.

"So then the cop had an interpreter question my sister, and that's when she supposedly said we'd had sex, or 'sexual relations,' as the cop put it."

Ms. LaRose is nodding, but I can't read the expression on her face. "Darcy," she says, "how would you feel about a face-to-face meeting with the girls, the interpreter and the police officer?"

"I'd feel great! Then I could find out why they said those things."

She nods. "That's what I thought. Someone guilty of sexually abusing little girls probably wouldn't agree to a meeting like that."

"I just don't know if the Kippensteins would agree to it, or if the cop will even let me see my sister."

"That's true. She may feel the girls will be too intimidated by your presence to talk freely."

"Sign freely, you mean."

"Oh. Right."

"But they won't be. You'll see." I feel my energy start to surge back. But then I hear the front door swing open, and Dad thumps up the stairs. He stops abruptly on the top step when he sees The Rose sitting at the kitchen table.

"Who the hell are you?" he demands. I see his eyes take in the huge hoop earrings and mass of cornrow braids that's she's been wearing lately. I can't wait to see his face when he notices her short skirt and leather boots.

She stands and reaches out her hand. "I'm Marie LaRose," she says. "Darcy's teacher."

"You're a teacher?" He shakes her hand, limply, but doesn't try to hide his astonishment.

"Yes, I am. I've brought Darcy his homework."

"Hmm." I can see he's still trying to get over her appearance. It's not often we have someone who looks so good in our townhouse. Come to think of it, this is probably a first.

"So, Darcy," she says, all businesslike again, "you've got your books, so you can get some work done to-night. And I'll see about arranging that meeting we talked about."

"Meeting?" Dad looks to me for an explanation.

Damn. I wish she hadn't said anything in front of him.

"That's right," Ms. LaRose tells him. "Darcy and I thought that it would be a good idea to meet with the girls, an interpreter, Samantha's parents and the police officer and discuss the…the situation."

"Darcy and you thought that, did you?"

"Yes. Yes, we did."

I see small red splotches appearing in Ms. LaRose's cheeks.

"Well, I think you can mind your own business," my dad tells her.

"This is my business. I'm his teacher."

"Your business is to teach him. You can stay the fuck out of his personal life."

"Pardon me?"

"You heard me. This has nothing to do with you."

"That's where you're wrong."

I don't know who would have won the standoff because the phone interrupts the glaring contest. Dad grabs the receiver.

"Hello!" he barks into it. He listens for one second and then says, "Darcy's not taking personal calls." He slams it down, but before he can go back to his glaring match it rings again.

"What!" He begins telling the caller off but abruptly pauses and listens.

"You can take the dog to the pound for all I care," he says. "Just stay away from here."

"Dad!"

Ms. LaRose must have decided that arguing with my dad is a no-win situation. She starts down the stairs. "Make sure you open your binder, Darcy," she says. "I've included an assignment that's due very soon."

"Right," I say, but I'm puzzled. There are never due dates attached to assignments when you're working at your own speed. There must be something else she wants me to see.

As soon as she's gone, Dad grabs a beer from the fridge and flicks on the TV. I head to my room with my books. I open up my journal first. Ms. LaRose has written today's quote on a fresh page.

To put the world in order, we must first put the nation in order; to put the nation in order, we must first put the family in order; to put the family in order, we must first cultivate our personal life; we must set our hearts right.—Confucius

I know one thing for sure; she's chosen this quote specifically for me. What she doesn't get is the fact there's no hope of putting my family in order. Well, maybe she'll get it now that she's met my dad. Sorry, Mr. Confucius, but I guess this means the world is screwed too.

I open my binder and find a sheet of paper folded inside it. I immediately recognize Gem's handwriting.

Hey Darcy,

What's happening? You looked like you were in a bit of trouble when I left you the other morning.

I've tried to call, but no one answers. I've still got Star, but I won't be able to keep her for long. I have to sneak her in and out of our townhouse complex (no dogs allowed) and my parents are freaked that we'll get evicted if I get caught with her. She's not the kind of dog you can hide under your coat. Tell me what to do!

I missed hangin' with you at lunch today.

—Gem

God. I missed hangin' with her too.

I lie on my bed for a while, thinking of Gem, of her face, of her soft brown hands, of her. As much as I hate to admit it, I like her. A lot. Way too much. And I like that she likes me.

It's been a day of acknowledgments. I think back to that scene with my mom, of remembering what really happened on that balcony ten years ago. How could I have forgotten something as important as that for so long? Had I really forgotten it? Did I block the memory of it somehow?

I sit up with a start. If I blocked the memory of Kat's fall so effectively, am I capable of blocking other things I've done…like sexually assaulting little girls? No!

And how is Kat going to feel when she finds out I am the one who dropped her? I bury my head back in my pillow. It is all too much to think about.

I long to get out my knife and purge these inner demons, but it's too soon. I have to let one set of wounds heal before I make any fresh cuts. That damn crying I did today actually seemed to give the same kind of relief, but a guy can't go around bawling his face off all the time. Cutting is the thing.

For lack of anything else to do, and being too restless to sleep, I tackle Ms. LaRose's quote. I write whatever comes to mind, knowing I don't ever have to show it to her if I don't want to.

How does a person go about cultivating his personal life? How do I set my heart right?

My personal life has only ever consisted of Kat and myself. Dad's given us the basics—shelter, food and clothes—but has he ever provided love? Is he capable of loving? How would Dad go about showing love if he did feel it? I can't even imagine. So even if I did "let my heart right" (whatever that means), I don't know if my family would ever be "in order." And Mom? Well that's another whole story. Order in this family? Not likely.

I guess you could say Sammy and her parents have been a part of my personal life. Especially Sammy. But now she's telling everyone that I hurt her. No, she's saying I sexually abused her. How will I ever set that right? Will she ever be part of my personal life again?

If I allow Gem into my life, is that a step toward cultivating my personal life? Will that set my heart right? How can it? With the memories I have to live with, how can my heart ever be set right?

Is there any hope for me?

I get up from my desk and stretch. Looking out my second-floor window to the street below, I visualize a much younger Kat, falling, falling, falling. Was she scared? Did I really believe she might land on her feet? She wasn't even walking yet.

Hate was far easier to live with than guilt.

Ten

Mom shows up early Tuesday morning. My heart sinks when I see her. I'm afraid she's come back to make me remember some other awful stuff from my childhood. It's Day Two of my self-imposed grounding.

"Not going to school again today?" she asks.

"Nope."

"Mind if I make some coffee then?" She investigates our kitchen by opening and closing cabinet doors.

"Fine with me, but you'll probably have to go buy some coffee beans first."

"Hmm." She holds up a small lumpy sack of something that she's pulled out of the far reaches of a hardly used cupboard. "Maybe I'll just have tea then."

I eye the lump that has now been identified as a tea bag. "Suit yourself," I tell her. "But none for me, thanks."

Mom regards the tea bag for a few more seconds. She tosses it in the garbage. "I wasn't really thirsty anyway," she says.

I flick on the TV and make myself comfortable on Dad's chair. She flops down on the sofa.

"Your sister's a wreck without you," Mom says over the drone of the TV.

That gets my attention. "She is?"

Mom nods. She says, very quietly, "I don't know if I can cope with her much longer."

"What's wrong with her?" I feel my alarm rising.

"It's her moods. Hysterical one moment and depressed the next. Between missing you and her dog... and she forgot her medicine on the weekend and then she had a seizure." She shakes her head. "I've got my own stuff to deal with. I can't deal with hers too."

"But you said you wanted her back."

"But I didn't know how hard it would be," she says.

"I doubt the cop will let her come back here...not now, anyway."

Mom gets up and starts pacing. I turn off the TV. "I'm just not used to so much responsibility," she says. "Weekends were fine. I was building up to it slowly. I think I could've done it if I'd been able to ease into it longer. For ten years I had people taking care of me. I don't know how to take care of someone else, though I'm trying to learn. But right now I'm feeling overwhelmed at the thought of having her full time."

Yesterday Mom seemed strong. Today I see her as the weakling she really is. I stand and face her, speaking right into her face. "You're overwhelmed? What about Kat? What about me? I've just found out that I tried to kill my sister when she was a baby. Now I'm being accused of sexually assaulting two little girls. Kat probably doesn't understand why she can't come home. And you're feeling overwhelmed?"

Mom sinks back down onto the sofa. I do the same in the chair. "Is there anyone else who could take her?" she asks.

"Only the Kippensteins, and under the circumstances, that doesn't seem like such a good idea, does it."

She hangs her head. I notice the sagging skin under her eyes.

"Are you doing drugs again, Mom?"

She shakes her head, but doesn't look up.

"Are you turning tricks?" I don't know why, but it feels good to accuse her of these things. Like we're getting even somehow.

"No!" she answers, her head jerking up. "I only did that to pay for the drugs!" I'm shocked at the defensive tone of her voice. "You have no idea what an addiction does to you, Darcy, what it forces you to do."

"You're right. I don't. But I did see what it did to you. That's enough to keep me off them."

"Well I'm glad I did something for you."

We sit quietly for a moment. I think about Kat and what I'd do to protect her, which is just about anything. "How hard is it to give her a pill each day?" I ask.

She looks me in the eye then. "She doesn't want me, Darcy. She wants you."

"Then why did she tell the cop we had sexual relations?"

Mom shakes her head. "She refuses to talk about that."

I flick the TV back on, disgusted with my mom. We stare at the screen for a while, but I doubt either of us is watching the show.

"Ms. LaRose said she'd try to set up a meeting with the girls and me. We could try to figure out what is going on."

Mom perks up. "She seems like a pretty cool teacher."

"Yeah, I guess she is." Imagine that. Me acknowledging that she's a good teacher. Go figure.

"Well, let me know."

"I will."

Mom gets up to leave. That's when I remember the other thing I need to talk to her about. "You sure you can't take Kat's dog for a while? My friend has her but she can't keep her any longer."

"Sorry, Darcy. There's no way."

I just nod and turn back to the TV. I hear the latch on the front door click.

THE PHONE RINGS around noon and I listen to the voice leaving a message on the answering machine.

"Darcy? Pick up the phone! It's me, Gem. Your dad won't let me talk to you but I've got to."

I pick it up and turn off the machine. "Hi, Gem."

"Darcy! What's going on?" I can't tell whether she's mad or worried. Maybe both. But what can I tell her?

That I've been accused of sexually assaulting two kids?

"I'm home with the flu or something."

"Oh. I thought maybe you'd gotten into trouble. There was that cop…"

"No. That was all sorted out. Just a misunderstanding." I hate lying to Gem like this.

"Then why didn't you take the dog back? Why won't your dad let you come to the phone?"

I never was a good liar. "Oh, that. Well Kat's at our mom's and Dad didn't want the dog. You know."

"No. I don't know. He thinks I should keep the dog every time your sister goes somewhere? What's going on, Darcy?"

I slump into a chair. I can't carry on this charade. "Okay, you're right. I am in trouble with Dad. Kat's away. I don't know why the dog can't come home. My dad's just got a wicked temper."

"What did you do?"

"I can't talk about that. But listen. Bring the dog over right after school. I'll hide her in my room or something. I'm sorry you got caught up in the middle of my problems."

"When does your dad get home from work?"

Good point. We don't need Dad finding Gem hanging around. "Okay. If the kitchen curtains are open, it's safe to bring Star in. If they're closed, it's not safe."

"Isn't he going to wonder why you're closing the curtains in the middle of the afternoon?"

She's right. I'm lousy at this kind of stuff. "All right. If the porch light is off, it's safe. I'll flick it on when he gets home. He won't notice from inside."

She's quiet for so long I begin to wonder if she's still there.

"Gem?"

"Yeah?"

"Thanks for keeping her for me."

"I wish I could keep her longer. She's so sweet. But my parents said that today is the last day. Besides, Star seems sad. I think she misses you."

Yeah right. "That would be Kat she's missing."

"You think so? I miss you."

I don't know what to say, so I don't say anything, but that doesn't mean I don't feel something. I feel a lot, but I don't know what to make of those feelings.

"Darcy?"

"Yeah?"

"You didn't say anything."

"I didn't know what to say."

"You could say thanks for having the dog."

"I already did."

"Okay, how about saying that you miss me too."

"I miss you too."

I can't believe I said it. My brain had wanted to, but my mouth and vocal chords wouldn't do the job. I'm so glad she put the words in my mouth, allowing them to spill out.

"I'm glad."

"Me too." Oh yeah. That was real cool.

She doesn't seem to notice. "Hopefully your dad won't be home after school so we can have a few minutes together."

"Yeah. Hopefully."

"Darcy?"

"Yeah?"

"You're not too good with words, are you."

"You noticed."

"That's okay. I can do the talking for both of us." She laughs, and I'm blown away by how wonderful the sound of her laughter is in my ear.

"See you later," she says.

"Later," I say.

It's the longest afternoon of my life. I pace the living room, watching out the window for Dad's car. I can't bear the thought of him coming home before Gem can bring the dog over.

Eventually I see Gem coming up the sidewalk with Star. I open the door and the dog gallops in, nearly knocking me over in her excitement to be home. I'm surprised at how happy I am to see her, too. It feels like a connection to Kat, pathetic as that is.

Gem and I stand awkwardly on the landing, watching Star charge up the stairs to look for Kat. I want to invite her in, yet I'm scared Dad will come home.

"I know I have to leave right away," she tells me.

"I'm sorry..."

Suddenly her hands are on my shoulders and she's

kissing my cheek. "Get back to school soon!" she says and slips back out the door.

I stand there, stunned. The only people who have ever kissed me before are Kat and Sammy. Maybe Mom did when I was little. I don't remember. I follow Star up the stairs and watch her sniff out each room. I realize I won't be able to keep Dad from finding out she's home. Right now I don't care. Gem kissed me.

Eleven

Don't ask me how she managed it, but she did. Ms. LaRose phoned to tell me the meeting between the girls, myself, the Kippensteins, an interpreter, a social worker and the cop is to take place Thursday afternoon, at the Kippensteins', as soon as Kat gets out of school. Apparently the girls were enthusiastic about seeing me, which is what made the cop and the newly appointed social worker agree to the meeting. They must have sensed that something wasn't quite right.

I spent all day Wednesday at home, agonizing over the meeting. Maybe I really did do what the girls said I did. After all, I had successfully blocked the memory of dropping Kat off the balcony. Had I forgotten again? Am I really a teenage pervert?

In the end, Dad didn't say much about Star's sudden reappearance. In fact, he isn't saying much of anything at all. He comes home from work, drinks beer in front of the TV and sleeps. Star and I may as well be invisible. He and Mom were informed of the meeting with the girls, but I'll be surprised if Dad shows. Kat is still with Mom, but I don't know how they are coping. I miss Kat so much. So does Star. We both spend a lot of time staring into space, pining for her.

The cop arrives Thursday afternoon to escort me to the Kippensteins'. When we pull into their driveway, I see The Rose's car, as well as a couple of unfamiliar ones. A sudden wave of panic grips me. What if the girls stick to their stories? What if they accuse me of doing those things to them in front of all these people? What if I suddenly remember that I really did do those things to them?

The cop is studying my face. "Ready?" she asks.

I draw in a long breath and nod. I follow her to the front door. She knocks lightly and then enters. Directly in front of us, in the living room, the "jury" awaits. The Kippensteins' sit together on the couch, holding hands. They won't look at me. Ms. LaRose and my mom, sitting on chairs, both smile brightly, but I can see they are forced smiles. The Rose is wearing a crisp white blouse with a scarf tied at her neck and a knee-length, navy blue skirt. Very conservative, yet I notice that she still looks as hot as ever. Maybe she just can't help herself.

There are two other women in the room. I'm quickly introduced to them. One is a social worker, the other an interpreter.

The cop indicates the chair that has been brought in for me. There is another one for her. I notice there is still an empty one, probably for Dad. Wishful thinking on their part.

There is no sign of the girls.

The cop starts the meeting. "We thought it best to hear from the girls one at a time, Darcy," she says. "They are in Samantha's bedroom waiting with a friend of Samantha's parents. They know we're all going to be here, but they don't know why. We just told them that we're going to be asking them some questions and that they need to answer as best they can."

I can only nod.

"I'll be asking the questions," she continues, looking around at the assembled group. "I'd appreciate it if the rest of you just listen quietly."

When no one says anything, she nods. "Okay, then, Ms. Murphy," she says to my mom. "Would you mind going and asking Katrina to join us?"

Mom nods and leaves the room. I spot Kat before she sees me. My heart thumps in my chest. It feels like years since I've seen her, and she looks pale and nervous. When she sees me her face lights up. "Darcy!" she says and rushes over. I automatically jump to my feet to greet her with a hug. I don't want to let her go. We hug for a long time. Eventually I sense Mom tugging Kat's arm and directing her to take a seat on the couch beside the Kippensteins. With a final squeeze for me, she crosses the room and plunks herself down.

"I can see you're happy to see your brother again," the cop says, and Denise, the interpreter, quickly relays the message.

Kat nods and smiles at me.

"Would you say you and your brother are very close?"

Kat looks puzzled. "Close?" she signs to the interpreter. "You mean we love each other a lot?"

"That's right," the cop says.

Kat nods. "Very close," she signs.

Now the cop nods. "And do you often share the same bed as your brother?" she asks.

Kat's fair skin turns crimson. "Sometimes I get scared at night," she signs slowly. "I don't like to be all alone so I climb in bed with Darcy. I know I'm getting too old to be scared, but I can't help it."

I feel the old heartache return. Kat shouldn't have to go through this, sharing her most embarrassing secrets in public. I feel my face burn.

"Katrina," the cop says quietly, "I now have to ask you some questions that may seem a little embarrassing, and you might feel uncomfortable giving me the answers, but it's very important that you do, and as honestly as you can."

Kat nods at the cop after watching Denise interpret, but she looks guarded.

"On March 14 you told an interpreter—not Denise but another one—that you had sexual relations with your brother."

I wouldn't have thought it possible, but Kat's face goes even redder and I see her eyes fill up with tears. She doesn't say anything.

"Is it true, Katrina?" the cop asks.

"I didn't say that," Kat signs, "because I don't really know what that means."

She might not know exactly what it means, but it is clear from her expression that she knows it's something embarrassing to talk about.

"Then what did you tell her?"

Katrina lets the tears spill. "That lady asked me if Darcy ever..." She begins to sob.

"If Darcy ever what, Katrina?"

Kat covers her face with her hands.

"Katrina?" the cop prompts, forgetting she can't hear her.

"I think she tricked me!" Kat suddenly signs wildly, her expression flipping from embarrassment to anger.

"I'd like you to finish that sentence, Katrina," the cop says. "She asked you if Darcy ever did what?"

It's hard to yell at a person when you're signing, but I think everyone in the room realizes that Kat is yelling with her hands. "She asked me if he'd ever touched me with his penis," she signs, glaring at the cop.

The cop remains unruffled. "And how did you answer her?" she asks.

Kat glances at me apologetically, then swipes at her tears before signing to the interpreter, "I told her that once, just once, Darcy's penis touched me, but she didn't let me explain that it was just an accident."

Now I feel my face go crimson. I'd put that morning out of my mind. That morning that I'd embarrassed myself so royally. I wish I could make myself invisible.

"How do you know it was an accident, Katrina?"

"I just do," she signs.

"Have you been taught about sex in school or by your parents?"

Kat shakes her head and looks down. I remember that Mrs. K was planning on getting Kat a book about puberty. I wish someone had given her a book on the facts of life.

"When two people are very close, Katrina," the cop says, "usually a husband and wife, but not always, the man puts his penis in a woman's vagina, and that is called sex."

I cannot believe this. For a split second I'm afraid she's about to launch into more detail, but fortunately she doesn't. I watch Kat's expression as she watches the interpreter. I feel mortified for her, but there is absolutely nothing I can do.

"You told us that you and Darcy are very close," the cop continues, "that you have a good relationship, so we think that maybe Darcy was having sex with you."

Kat jumps to her feet, her head shaking from side to side. "It wasn't like that," she signs. Mrs. Kippenstein reaches up and pulls Kat, very gently, back down onto the couch.

"Are you sure you're not just trying to protect your brother, Katrina, the brother you love so much?"

God. Enough already.

I've never seen Kat so steamed about anything. She's usually a perfect little lady, but right now I'm worried she might spit at the cop or reach over and rip out her hair or something.

"I got into his bed and I was really cold so I cuddled up to him," she signs rapidly. She waits while the interpreter repeats this. "It poked me once and I jumped out of bed. He didn't mean anything. He said he was sorry."

I'm acutely aware of people glancing at me, looking for my reaction. I stare at a stain on the carpet.

The cop thanks Kat for her honesty and then asks her to return to Samantha's room. Again Kat throws me an apologetic glance. I just nod and do my best to give an encouraging smile.

Mrs. K brings little Sammy in next and she wiggles in between her parents on the couch. She grins and waves at me. I wave back. Poor little thing, she couldn't have a clue about what is going on.

The cop starts off by asking Sammy, via the interpreter, if I'm a nice baby-sitter. She nods enthusiastically. Then the cop goes for the jugular. "Has someone, not Mommy or Daddy or the doctor, but someone else recently touched you in a place that is usually under your bathing suit?"

It takes the interpreter a couple of attempts to get the question across to Sam, but when she does, her reaction is painful to watch. She turns and presses her face into Mrs. K's chest, and you can see the little shoulders heaving with her sobs. Mrs. K hugs her close.

"I think her reaction is the answer you're looking for," Mr. K says.

The cop nods in agreement.

Finally Sammy calms down enough to face the room again, but her thumb is firmly planted in her mouth. For a change, her mom doesn't pull it out.

"Can you tell us who hurt you in those private places, Sammy?" the cop asks.

Sammy seems to think for a moment before she answers. Then, to my horror, she signs the letter D. The interpreter translates this to the cop. My heart bangs in my chest. Sammy has clearly named me as the abuser, she is traumatized by the memory of the abuse, yet she was delighted to see me when she came into the room.

What the hell is going on?

"Is this person, this D person, in the room today, Sammy?" the cop asks.

I don't breathe as I watch the interpreter translate this to her.

You can see—by the expression on her face—the exact moment Sammy comprehends this question. Her wide eyes look around the room again, frightened, as if perhaps she missed someone, and then she shakes her head. "No," she says, very, very clearly.

"Are you sure?" the cop asks.

She nods, her little face pale.

"But I thought you used the letter D to refer to Darcy," she says, gesturing at me.

I watch as the interpreter tries to explain this to Sam. A look of horror crosses Sammy's face when she realizes what she is being told. Her hands start to sign quickly, more quickly than I've ever seen her sign before. "D is at the start of his name," she says, pointing at me, "but it also starts my uncle's name."

Mrs. K gasps.

"What is her uncle's name?" the cop asks Mrs. K.

Mrs. K is visibly shocked. Her face is as pale as Sammy's and I can see her hand is shaking as she pushes her hair behind her ear. "David," she says quietly. "His name is David."

David is Sammy's uncle, the one who baby-sits her on Saturdays.

Sammy buries her face in her mom's chest again, and Mrs. K lays her head on the top of her daughter's.

The cop turns to me, obviously embarrassed. "We owe you an apology, Darcy," she says. "I'm sorry, very sorry, that we put you through this."

I'm too numb to speak. I just nod.

And then everyone is standing and Ms. LaRose is hugging me, hard. I guess it's okay for her to hug me when we're not alone. Wiping my eyes, I can't help but wonder where these tears were hiding for the first fifteen years of my life. Now that they've come unleashed, they seem to be making an appearance every day. Just making up for lost time I guess.

A lot of hugging goes on for the next ten minutes. After Ms. LaRose, I find myself in my mom's embrace. Then it's Kat, who has been allowed out of the bedroom. I see Ms. LaRose hugging my mom. Then I find myself standing in front of Mr. Kippenstein. He places his hand on my shoulder. "I'm sorry, Darcy," he says, very seriously. "We made a terrible mistake."

I can only nod. Now that the tears have appeared, my voice has gone into hiding. Mrs. K has disappeared from the room, followed by the cop.

"I hope you'll be able to forgive us."

Nod nod. Sniff sniff. It's the best I can do.

I FIND OUT later that it's often a family member who is responsible in sexual abuse cases. Of course in this case it was much easier to lay the blame on the screwed-up, antisocial, teenaged baby-sitter whose mom was just released from the slammer for attempted murder. Gee, even I might have suspected me.

I'm told that Sammy's uncle will see true justice done once he's in prison. Even prisoners don't like child molesters.

I hope that's true.

I'm alone now, alone with my knife and my old towel. This time there's not an overwhelming need to cut. This time it's because I want to cut. The knife is my old friend. And besides, it's easier to cut than not cut.

I lower the knife to my skin and press, feeling its sharp edge slice my skin, drawing a thread-like line of blood. The knife crosses my arm. It's been a horrible week. First it was that scene with my mom and rediscovering my guilt in Kat's fall. I draw another line, and another. Then there was that horrible meeting today, at the Kippensteins'. Sure, Sammy proved that I was innocent, but not until I'd been thoroughly messed up. I keep on slicing. The cuts become deeper and more erratic as I get worked up, rehashing the events of the week. Before I know it, my arm is a slashed-up mess and I'm feeling ashamed, angry and confused. I'm also starting to feel a little woozy, almost delirious. I keep on cutting, hacking away desperately, no longer worried about cleaning up the blood.

I WAKE UP in the dark, disorientated and cold. I must have passed out onto the floor. Kat is leaning over me, shaking me awake. I feel a cold nose sniffing the back of my neck. I hear Kat pad back to the door, and she flicks on the overhead light. We both flinch at the harsh light, and then she looks down at me, gasps, horrified, and puts both hands over her mouth.

I look down on myself to see what she's seeing.

It is an ugly sight. Blood is everywhere. My towel, on the floor beside me, is soaked, and there's a dark stain in the old carpet. My shirt and pants are ruined. I glance at my arm and have to look away. It looks like it's been through a meat grinder and it's throbbing hard. Star starts to lick at it but I give her a shove.

"We have to get you to the hospital," Kat signs.

"No!" I drag myself to my feet, feeling dizzy and nauseous. "I'll clean everything up. It's okay. It looks worse than it is."

She eyes me, unconvinced.

"Really, Kat. If anyone finds out they'll…" I don't finish the sentence. I don't know what they'd do.

She looks me in the eye for a long time. Finally she signs, "I'll help you clean up."

I sigh with relief. "I can do it, Kat, no problem. I'll go clean up my arm first and then I'll take care of everything else. You go back to bed."

"Can I sleep in your bed?" she asks, sheepishly.

I think about that. "No," I say. "You can't."

She nods, understanding. "C'mon, Star," she says, and with a last sad look at me, they leave the room.

Twelve

M s. LaRose asks me to stay after school. I wait while the others leave the classroom and then join her at the back table. I must be coming down with the flu or something. All afternoon I've been fluctuating between chills and sweats. My arm throbs. I give a little tug on my sleeve, making sure the gauze bandage is covered.

"You okay, Darcy?" The Rose asks. "You look a little pale."

"I think I'm just getting a cold or something."

She studies me. "Your eyes are glassy too. Are you sure you're okay?"

"Yeah. I'll be fine." But I'm beginning to wonder myself.

"Okay," she nods. "Now, what I wanted to know is if things are getting back to normal for you," she says.

"Normal?" I ask. "Like living with a dad who doesn't want kids, and having an ex-convict for a mom who can only cope with being a parent in short spurts? Yep, things are pretty much back to normal."

Okay, I admit I feel a little guilty saying that about my mom, but the words just spilled out of my mouth. It must be the fever.

She nods. "Well then," she says finally, "I'm thinking of recommending to Mr. Bryson that you return to the regular system. I don't think there's any reason you need to continue at Hope Springs Alternate School."

Wham. That came out of nowhere. I'm feeling dizzier by the moment, and I have no idea how to respond, but I know one thing for sure: There's no way I'm returning to the regular system. For the first time I realize how much I like it here; Ms. LaRose is my savior and, more importantly, this is where Gem is. "So what do I have to do to keep my spot here?" I ask.

"Oh, that would be easy," she says. "You just have to convince your teacher that you're not nearly ready to go back."

"I'm not nearly ready to go back."

"That's not very convincing," she says, smiling.

"Okay," I say. I'm beginning to see stars in the air between us, but I have to think. I wipe the sweat off my forehead with my left arm and then notice The Rose staring at it. I glance down and see that my sleeve has worked its way up again and the bandage is showing.

"What happened to your arm?" she asks.

In that moment I realize that the cutting may be my ticket to staying here, but I'm too ashamed to admit what I do, especially to The Rose. And besides, I'm having to really concentrate to stay focused.

"Can we talk tomorrow?" I ask her, finding myself trembling again. "I'm really not feeling well."

I see The Rose jumping to her feet and coming around the table toward me. The next thing I know I'm flat out on the floor, and when I look up, for a split second I think I see an angel hovering there. Then I realize it's just Ms. LaRose looking down on me. Great, now I'm hallucinating too.

"Whoa, sorry," I say, struggling to sit up.

She pushes me back down. "Stay still," she says. "I've just called an ambulance."

"You have?" Where was I when she was doing that? "It's just the flu," I tell her, but I don't bother to try sitting up again. It's way too much effort.

I VAGUELY RECALL being put on a stretcher and then into an ambulance. The Rose stays with me all the way to hospital. I float in and out of consciousness.

I wake with a start when I feel someone unraveling the gauze I've wrapped around my arm. I try to pull it away, but it's too late.

"Oh my God!" I hear Ms. LaRose exclaim.

I can't look at her, but I do glance at the nurse who is examining my arm. "Self-inflicted?" she asks coolly.

I try to pull my arm away, but she hangs on and it's too painful to pull hard. I refuse to answer though.

"Darcy?" Ms. LaRose asks.

I won't answer her either.

"Well it's badly infected," the nurse says, "and that's why you're sick. As soon as I can get the consent from your parents I'll get an IV started, because I expect the doctor will put you on a course of antibiotics. You've really done a number on yourself," she adds.

She puts my arm down and leaves the cubicle, pulling the curtain shut behind her. I close my eyes, trying to avoid Ms. LaRose's questions.

She picks up the hand of my good arm. "Why, Darcy?" she asks.

"Just because," I say, without opening my eyes.

I'M HOOKED UP to an IV, I'm in a room with two little kids and I'm totally bored. I've been in the hospital for four days now, and the medicine must be working because I'm feeling fine, my arm no longer feels like it's on fire and I want to get the hell out of here.

"When do I get to leave?" I ask a nurse who's taking the temperature of the boy in the bed across the room from me. He's just had his tonsils removed.

"Hey, if it was up to me, I'd have sent you home days ago," she says.

"So why don't you tell the doctor that?"

"Because he's obligated to try to get you well."

"And you're not?"

She writes something on the boy's chart. "There are lots of really sick people for me to care for, and people who have been in accidents that were no fault of their own. You, on the other hand…"

She doesn't finish her sentence. She doesn't have to.

Ms. LaRose pokes her head into the lounge where I'm watching TV, my trusty IV pole standing at attention beside me.

"Can I come in?" she asks.

"It's a free world."

"So," she says, sitting down beside me, "I've done some reading on SI."

"On what?"

"SI, short for Self Injury."

"Oh. And what did you find out? That I'm crazy?"

"No, I'm afraid you won't be able to use craziness as an excuse."

"Bummer. Then what excuse can I use?"

"How about…" she reads from the pad of paper she's carrying, "'Feelings of overwhelming tension and isolation derived from fear of abandonment, self-hatred and apprehension'."

"That's why people cut themselves?"

"Some people."

I keep my eyes glued to the TV, trying not to act too interested, but intrigued nonetheless.

"What about the rest?"

"There's lots of reasons." She refers to her notes again. "It's a complex coping behavior. It can be an expression of emotional pain, an escape from emptiness or depression, or a release of anger."

"Yeah, but why do those things make a person want to carve their skin?"

"I'm sure you could answer that better than me."

"Maybe, but what do the experts say?" I ask.

She picks her notes up again and reads, "'There is evidence that when dealing with strong emotions or overwhelming situations, self-injurers harm themselves because it brings them a quick release from tension and anxiety. It is a means of coping with an overpowering psycho-physiological arousal'."

The word "release" jumps out at me. That's about all I understand. "So what's the cure?"

"There is no cure, Darcy."

"I can look forward to mutilating myself for the rest of my life? Great."

"There is no cure, Darcy, but you can stop anytime you want."

"Oh, yeah, easy for you to say."

"Can we turn that thing off?" The Rose asks, referring, irritably, to the TV. I guess she doesn't care for talk shows where the host and audience badger the deviant guest until they get a good reaction. Before she arrived I was beginning to think I'd make a good candidate, showing the world my mutilated arm and talking about the thrill I get when I cut myself. Of course, I'd use the word thrill, not release. It sounds more, well, deviant.

"You have to replace the cutting with other ways of releasing the bad feelings," The Rose continues after the TV goes off.

"Ahh," I say. "I get it now. I could use drugs, like my mom did. Or numb myself with booze every night, like Dad. Perfect. Thanks, Ms. LaRose, you've been a big help. Do you mind if I turn the TV back on?"

I hate the hurt look on The Rose's face, but I can't help myself.

Of course, The Rose is not easily put off. As usual, she turns things around. "That's interesting, Darcy, that you can see the similarities in your mom and dad's behavior with your own."

Oh, puh-leese.

"And I understand your mom has given up drugs. What do you think she replaced them with?"

"That's different. She was forced to give up drugs. She was in prison, remember? They don't sell drugs there. Not in the unit she was in, anyway."

"Has she started again?"

"You'd have to ask her."

"What do you think?"

I can only shrug. "I don't think so, but I bet she's thought of it."

"I quit smoking five years ago," The Rose says, "and I still think of it occasionally, but it doesn't mean I'll start again."

"Then what do you think my mom has replaced it with?"

"Well, it's just a guess," she ventures, "but I'd say honesty and talking about her feelings is one way she's worked through it."

"Are you saying I'm not honest?"

She sighs. "Darcy, you really can be difficult, can't you."

I don't answer. I know she's right.

She folds her papers and puts them in her purse.

"I have to go," she says, "but I suggest you give some thought to what we've just talked about."

"Yes, Dr. LaRose."

She scrunches up her face, trying to look nasty, and then laughs. "Oh, Darcy, what am I going to do with you?"

I don't tell her, but the truth is, she's already done a whole lot. The fact that she hasn't just given up on me is amazing enough.

"It's hopeless," I tell her. "I suggest you quit while you're ahead."

"Not on your life," she says, leaving the room.

A PSYCHIATRIST VISITS me before I'm released from the hospital. He doesn't say much, except to tell me that SI is not usually an indication of suicidal behavior, so as a result I don't have to be put on a suicide watch. I do have to set up an office appointment with him, though, but that's it. The earliest he can see me is two weeks from now.

It's a good thing I'm not suicidal.

I FIND MY STATUS at home and school has changed somewhat now that the world knows about my habit of inflicting injury on myself. Dad is making an effort to be a little nicer, a little more attentive, and Mom, when I see her, which isn't often, looks at me knowingly, her eyes full of sympathy.

The kids at school want to see my scars and then act impressed. Even Troy. Believe me, impressing them is not the idea. Far from it.

The Kippensteins continue to beg for forgiveness for wrongfully accusing me of abusing Sam. They've bought me gifts and they've even talked about setting up a trust fund for me, for my education or something. I keep telling them it's okay, I'd probably have done the same thing. I can't imagine how it must feel to know someone has hurt your little girl like that. You wouldn't be able to think straight. Actually, I can imagine. If someone had hurt Kat that way...

I'm no longer employed by the Kippensteins. Mrs. K has taken a leave of absence from work. I promised Sammy that Kat and I (and Star) would still drop in a couple of times a week to play with her.

And Star. It turns out she's not only a chick-magnet (Gem), but she's everything Kat hoped she'd be, and more. As Kat grows, and especially now, during puberty, she often has to have her medication adjusted. When she returned home from Mom's she began having regular seizures again. It only took a few before Star learned to sense them coming moments before they actually hit. She would use all her guide dog training to protect Kat during the seizure. In the meantime, Kat's had her dosage changed and she's fine again. And another interesting development. It turns out that Dad is way better with dogs than he is with kids. He still hasn't learned much sign language, but while I was in the hospital he did get that dog trained to take Kat her bottle of medication before she (the dog) got her morning ration of food.

I THINK GEM has taken me on as her personal pet project, and I admit, I don't mind a bit. She often comes home with me after school, and we walk the dog with Kat. Gem is learning to sign, and Kat is having a great time teaching her. I still haven't had the nerve to show Gem my appreciation that she's a nonsmoker, but I'm hoping that will come soon.

I noticed that my knife was gone from my room when I got out of the hospital. No biggie. It's easy to replace. The stain on my carpet is a constant reminder of the night I got carried away. I won't let that happen again. Control is the key.

I WATCH AS KAT tucks her purse into her backpack and remember the day she bought it. That seems like ages ago, but it's really only been about six weeks. I make a mental note to tell Mom to talk to her about girl things, periods and who knows what else. It's a relief to be let off the hook when it comes to that stuff.

Once again Star and I see her off to school from the top step before I pick up the newspaper and return to the kitchen, where my unfinished breakfast is still sitting on the table. I made omelets today, scrambled eggs yesterday. Somehow breakfast has now become one of my responsibilities.

With a sense of foreboding, I open the paper and scan the editorial page. Today there are only two letters condemning Mom, but that's still two letters too many. Sometimes I wonder how she can take it, this continuous slander for something she didn't do. She still tells me that going to prison really was the best thing that could have happened to her. I'm trying hard to believe that, I really am, and I might be able to live with it if I didn't keep thinking about what could have happened to Kat. That's when I get feeling really bad. That's also when I think about replacing my knife.

KAT IS BACK to doing weekend visits with Mom, so Gem and I are at the creek, alone, throwing sticks for Star. Until now, Gem hasn't asked about the cutting, and I haven't said anything, but seeing as she wants to be my co-savior with The Rose, I knew the topic would come up eventually.

"So why do you cut yourself?" she asks, glancing down at my arm. I realize I've been stroking the new scars again, unconsciously.

"Well, The Rose says it's because it…" I do my best LaRose imitation, "brings release from tension and anxiety."

"What would The Rose know about it?"

"She's a teacher, remember? She does research." There goes my alter ego again, the one who can't help being sarcastic.

"C'mon, Darcy." She doesn't appreciate my sense of humor. "Why do you do it?"

I look at the new scars more closely. The swelling has gone down and they've faded to a light pink color. "I guess she's right. It does bring release."

"Well I get tense and anxious sometimes too, you know," she says. "But I don't start cutting myself."

"Then what do you do?"

She thinks about that. "I yell at my brother, eat junk food, you know, the usual stuff."

"I don't have a brother to yell at, and eating doesn't do anything but fill me up. Any other suggestions?"

"Yell at your sister."

"Nah."

"Take the dog for a walk."

"Wouldn't work."

"Well there must be something!"

"I haven't found anything as good yet."

We walk along in silence for a while. I guess fixing me isn't going to be as easy as she thought.

"So what makes you tense and anxious?" she asks.

That's an easy one. "People."

"What people?"

"Most people. Not you. Not Kat or The Rose. But just about everyone else."

"It's kind of hard to avoid people."

"You're catching on."

She doesn't answer. I regret being so flippant and decide to open up to her, a little.

"And now there's something else."

"What?" she asks cautiously, wondering if I'm about to jerk her around some more.

"The shit my mom's going through."

She chucks a stick ahead of us for Star to chase. "It wasn't that long ago you figured she deserved it. You said you didn't care."

"Yeah, well, that was because I didn't know everything." Oops, that was more than I meant to say.

"Oh." I can see the hesitation on her face. She wants to pry, but she doesn't know if she should.

I decide to make it easy on her. Just talking to her about this makes me feel better. "Gem." I stop walking and she turns to face me.

"What?"

"I'm going to tell you something, but there's a good chance you'll hate me afterwards."

She smiles at that. "Yeah right."

There's no turning back now. It occurs to me that I've just taken a huge gamble without any thought of what could happen. For the first time in my life I've made a friend, and a girl friend at that, and now I risk losing her. But something, some demon, has taken over my usually rational mind and I drop the bomb. "My mom, she didn't do it."

"Do it?" The questioning smile begins to fade from her face.

"I did. I dropped Kat from that balcony."

She stares at me, her mouth gaping. "Holy shit."

"I told you you'd hate me."

She stares at me some more. "Darcy! You were only four years old!"

"Yeah, but I must have a killer instinct."

"Is that what you think?"

"Yeah. Duh."

"Get a grip, Darcy. At four you wouldn't know better! You were just a little boy. You probably saw one too many cartoons where a person would hit the pavement and bounce right back up, good as new."

"Whatever. I still did it."

She's studying me, looking stunned. I'd feel stunned too if someone told me they did such a thing.

"You've got to get over this, Darcy," she says. "You can't go on feeling guilty."

"Yeah right, Gem." Now I'm feeling a little ticked. She doesn't get it. "Look at what could have happened to Kat! She could have been killed. And my mom! She went to prison for ten years to protect me. Wouldn't that make you feel just a little bit guilty, Gem?"

"No," she says, sounding mad. "Your mom was the screwup, not you."

"You're right there," I agree, still angry. "My mom was a screwup, but she didn't attempt to murder her own kid like everyone says."

"Then deal with that! But get over what happened. It's done, Kat's fine and you're the best brother in the whole world. Believe me. I have a brother and I know that the relationship you have with Kat is not typical."

That word "relationship" makes me squirm. Too many people have implied things with it, yet for some reason Gem's comment makes me feel a little better. I have been a good brother. I know I have.

"Then how do you suggest I deal with my mom getting tormented for something she didn't do?"

"Tell the world the truth—that you did it."

"You're crazy!"

"Why?"

"Because—" But I can't finish the sentence. The real truth is too ugly. I could live with the rest of the world knowing what I did, but not with Kat knowing. How could she ever forgive that? Look at how I hated Mom all those years. Kat would feel the same way about me.

It's getting dark and we turn and begin the return trip home in silence. We walk single file along the creekside path, but once we climb back up to the field, Gem takes my hand and holds it tightly the rest of the way home.

She'll never know how much that means to me.

Just when I'd begun to think The Rose is an okay teacher, she's ticked me off again. All those quotes I missed when I was away? She copied them all into my journal and now she says I have to respond to them. All of them. I've put it off, hoping she'd forget, but now she says she wants them by Monday morning.

It's late and Dad's asleep when I sit down at my desk with a pen and my school journal open in front of me. A serrated steak knife with a sharp tip sits beside them. I have no idea what I will reach for first.

I read through the quotes again. The Rose has made no attempt to hide the fact that these were chosen for my benefit. I wonder if the other kids ever even saw them.

The first one is the most obvious.

Other things may change us, but we start and end with family.—Anthony Brandt

The next one is kind of horrifying when you think about it.

Don't hold your parents up to contempt. After all you are their son, and it is just possible you may take after them.— Evelyn Waugh

Finally, there's a change of topic.

Truth, like surgery, may hurt, but it cures.—Han Suyin

I hold the pen over the paper, then put it down. This is so easy for her! She probably has a perfectly normal family, a family that has Sunday night dinners together each week and that gathers for birthdays and Christmas. Sure, she can easily imagine taking after them!

Ripping out the page with LaRose's fancy handwriting on it, I crumple it into a ball and chuck it across the room.

I pick up the knife and study my arm. There's not much skin left that isn't crisscrossed by fine white lines. I hold my arm under the glow of the desk lamp and study the scars more closely. God. My arm has been the battlefield for all those inner wars that have raged inside me over the years. I've bled and bled again, but each time those blood platelets surged to the rescue and my skin healed, leaving this labyrinth of scars. I touch the point of the knife to my arm. I push it a little harder, wondering how hard I'd have to press with this knife to break the surface. Then I put the knife down and lay my head on my desk.

I don't want to bleed anymore. I want it to be over. What did Gem say I should do? Tell the world the truth, the truth about what I did? Is that what I need to do?

I pick the crumpled wad of paper off the floor and flatten it out on my desk. *Truth, like surgery, may hurt, but it cures.*

I've denied myself the truth for ten years—ten whole years of suppressing it, and it did fester inside me, making me crazy. The cutting was the only way I knew to bring the pain to the surface. But now I know the truth.

Tell the world the truth.

I pick up my pen and start to write.

Epilogue

After recovering from her initial tongue-tying, mind-blowing shock, Ms. LaRose was totally enthusiastic about me writing a confession letter for the *Hope Springs Daily*. She even helped me write it and agreed that I could do it instead of "responding" to her stupid quotes. I admit, it was scary and I almost withdrew it at the last minute, but then I didn't.

It has been the most amazing experience.

It ran a month ago, but the letters to the editor continue to trickle in. It turns out that the community is forgiving after all. I'm stunned by the support, actually. Who would have guessed? People recognize me on the street and say hi and then ask me how I'm doing. I'm even told that I've become something of a local hero for coming forward publicly with my confession. Word of my si reached a bunch of local organizations and I've been asked to write personal experience pieces for some journals and even to speak at events. It's flattering, but I've turned them all down. It's not something I want to be considered an expert on.

I almost got an ulcer worrying that Kat would hate me when she found out the truth. I should have known better. She pointed out that when I did the horrible thing I was the same age Sammy is now, and that has helped me begin to forgive myself. Four-year-olds really can't be held responsible for all their actions. Besides, I think she finds it a relief to know that her mom didn't do it.

At first Mom was ticked right off by my newspaper-letter confession. She didn't want to be seen as a martyr, but now that she knows how much it's helped me deal with my guilt, she's come around to seeing why I had to do it. She takes it upon herself to do a weekly arm check on me. I let her, partly because I know it makes her feel like she's being a responsible parent (I consider it my contribution to her ongoing therapy) and partly because I like the feeling of having a mom, even if it is a little late in the game. So far she hasn't spotted any new cuts, but I'm not making any promises. I haven't felt that overwhelming need to cut lately, but if I do, you never know. Maybe I've done what The Rose suggested—found other coping devices. I guess that acknowledging the truth was the biggie, and maybe I no longer feel the need to punish myself.

Speaking of Mom, she's now working at Kat's school as a secretary. I think it was knowing sign language that landed her the job, and having me clear her name publicly didn't hurt either. Aside from the arm checks, we don't get together often, but when we do, we get along okay. I realize now how much she must have loved me all those years ago. Accepting that prison term for something she didn't do proves it. I might never have understood the significance of that if I didn't now know firsthand the rage of injustice at being falsely accused of something.

Kat still spends weekends with Mom and, of course, sees her every day at school. She's made it clear that she sees this as a permanent arrangement. I don't think you can say my sister's chosen Star over Mom, but she's found this to be a compromise that works for everyone, even Dad, or so it seems. Gosh, maybe this family is finding some kind of order after all. What do you think of that, Mr. Confucius? Today my family, tomorrow the world!

GEM AND I STOPPED by the Kippensteins' after school today to play with Sammy, but Sam made it perfectly clear that who she really wanted to see was Star. Gem offered to go get her, but when she returned she was short one dog.

"You forgot something," I told her.

"I got there too late."

"Too late for what?"

"Your dad took off with her."

"He did? In his car?" My heart flip-flopped in my chest. Could he have decided to return her after all this time? He's always complaining about the cost of feeding her, the vet bills, the hair on the carpet. It wouldn't take much for him to suddenly lose it—a puddle of piddle on the floor maybe, or a chewed corner on the couch—and he'd haul her back where she came from.

"No," Gem assured me. "Not in his car. He took her for a walk."

"Dad's walking Star?"

Gem nods.

"Huh." Imagine that. Dad walking Star. The world is full of surprises.

And then it hits me. Star's a chick-magnet. Dad's not so stupid after all.

Maybe hope does spring daily.

THE TRUTH ABOUT SHERRI MURPHY

BY DARCY MURPHY FRASER

Sherri Murphy, the woman convicted of dropping her baby daughter off the balcony of her fifth floor apartment, didn't do it. I did. I am her son.

No, this is not a joke. I was just four years old at the time, but I do remember the day. I remember thinking that because my sister's name was Kat, she should land on her feet, but of course that is not what happened.

I am writing this letter because I can no longer sit back and watch my mom take the blame for something she didn't do. She went to prison to protect my innocence. She has never intentionally hurt anyone—except herself—but I have. I hurt my whole family by dropping Kat off that balcony, and I've continued to inflict injury on myself. My hope is that by facing the truth of my actions, I too will be able to heal.

Thank you.

Shelley Hrdlitschka's last teen novel, *Dancing Naked*, was an ALA Quick Pick and an ALA Best Book nominee, a finalist for the CLA YA Book Award and winner the OLA White Pine award. Shelley lives in North Vancouver, British Columbia.